USA TODAY BESTSELLING AUTHOR

DALE MAYER

DARKEST DESIGNS

BOOK 3 OF THE DESIGNS TRILOGY

About This Book

Drawing is her world…but when she's pushed into the In-Between and thought lost forever, it's his world too.

Her… Storey doesn't want to become a living dead lost In-between. She thought she'd known the worst that could happen…but she wasn't even close. ey Dalton wants her life back. Her home back. Her world back. The way they were before she messed with time. She does not want.

Him… Eric thought he'd seen the worst that his father could do…but he hadn't…unfortunately. Heartbroken and panicked, Eric tracks Storey to the misty dead space – and follows her in. There is a way out – but not a way that anyone would willingly choose.

It… The stylus has no way to help with Storey's latest predicament. But survival is paramount. Only this time it can't do it alone. There might be help available…if they can save someone else…first.

Them… Storey wants to save her world. Eric wants to save Storey. The stylus wants them to save someone else. But can anyone save them all?

Sign up to be notified of all Dale's releases here!
https://geni.us/DaleNews

Acknowledgments

Darkest Designs wouldn't have been possible without the support of my friends and family. Many hands helped with proofreading, editing, and beta reading to make this book come together. I had a vision, but it took many people to make that vision real. I thank you all.

PROLOGUE

In Deadly Designs we let off with this chapter…

S OMEONE MOANED.

Storey wished they'd stop. Her headache boomed deep inside. "Easy, Storey." Eric's voice split right through her skull. She shuddered.

"It's over now, but we almost didn't make it. We're still feeling the effects of their telepathic weapon."

Storey sat up in a panic, grabbing her head as it threatened to explode. "Did the portal come with us?"

The large sheet of paper landed in the dirt in front of her. Groaning, she dropped back to the ground and picked up the paper. "Thank heavens. I don't think I'd be able to run anywhere right now."

"Too bad," snapped an angry voice behind them. "You took so long to get here, we don't have a choice. We have to leave now."

Storey closed her eyes. Damn. The Councilman still lived.

"Hello, father." Eric struggled to his feet.

Storey didn't bother. Besides, she wasn't sure she could. The pounding inside her skull had eased slightly, but not enough to make movement a good idea yet.

"Storey? You can recuperate back home."

Home? Her eyelids popped open. "That much effort

might be possible."

"Better yet," the Councilman snapped, "we leave you here. You're responsible for this mess. Let's go, Eric."

"No." Eric's harsh voice left no doubt about his seriousness. "She comes with us or I leave you here."

Storey's gaze landed on the Councilman's face long enough to see the hate glazing his eyes. He obviously hadn't come to terms with her presence in his world. At least back at Paxton's lab, she knew they'd take care of him. With false energy, she struggled to her feet, but was forced to stay bent over for a long moment to adjust to being vertical.

"Can you see any of the other codexes? Portals?" She studied around the dark space. It appeared empty. But in the darkness, who could tell for sure? And they didn't have time for a full search right now.

"Father, did they leave anything here with you?"

"No, they didn't understand and ruined the portals with water. They are wearing the codexes. That's how they went home." He snorted as he scrambled to his feet. "They didn't need much guidance on their usage."

Storey exchanged an appalled look with Eric. How much did the Louers know of Toran technology after their session with Eric's father? "If Paxton can shut them down that might be the easiest way to deal with any that can't be retrieved."

"And if he can't?" Eric glared at his father. "Did you really help them use the codexes…against your own people?" His jaw worked furiously. "Have you so little regard for your home? That you would bring something like this on them?"

The Councilman turned his back on Storey to glower at Eric. He sniffed hard and lifted his nose into the air. "It was the only way to secure my safety."

"Jesus," Storey muttered under her breath. "Eric, are you

prepared to trust his word about the portals and codexes?"

Running a hand through his short cropped hair, Eric frowned. He walked the small space where his father had been held. There were small pieces of paper on the ground at the doorway to the next cavern, soaked and damaged beyond use. "He's correct about these." Eric pointed to the fragments. "Let's hope Paxton *can* disable the remaining codexes."

Storey walked over, the portal in her hand. "I'll ask the stylus to disable any still functioning portals as well. Soon as we get somewhere safe."

"That makes sense."

"Enough already," snapped the Councilman. "The guards will be here any minute. Let's go."

Even as the words left his mouth they heard heavy sounds of someone running. Then another set of running footsteps.

"Shit." Storey stepped back to give Eric room. "Hurry."

Eric bent over in agony, his hands clasped to his ears.

"My head. The pain. I can't think."

That same horrible noise built up inside Storey's head. Damn the Louers' and their secret weapon. "We have to go. Punch the codes." Storey gasped as the pain increased.

"Hurry up," snapped the Councilman. The noise twisted his features, but didn't seem to be crippling him the same as Eric and her. "Why can't we travel by portal?"

Time. That's why they couldn't go by portal. "It has to be codex. Time is a problem with portals." Storey yelled to be heard over the pounding in her head.

Eric's gaze widened as he understood her. "Right. I forgot." He took a deep breath, pulled back his sleeve and tapped a sequence of numbers.

The Councilman stepped closer, his nervous gaze searching the darkness around them. Hissing, he said, "Hurry."

"It takes a moment." Eric's face twisted against the unbearable noise. He bent over gasping for breath. Mist swirled up from the ground. Storey struggled to remain conscious as pain turned her world black. She didn't know how Eric was faring or why the Councilman seemed unaffected. Unless his sheer size had something to do with it.

Gratefully, she realized that the higher the black mist, the less the noise penetrated. It didn't take long before she could stand up straight. Over Eric's shoulder she watched several Louer guards race into the chamber. "Uh, Eric? How far does the mist have to climb before it's too late to reverse?"

She nodded behind him. He turned his head, his shoulders relaxed. "It's too late now."

The Councilman glared at her. "Don't be telling her any of our secrets."

"It's hardly a secret, Father. Besides, it's nothing to what you've told them."

Keeping a wary eye on the two Louers, Storey held her breath until the mist blocked her view. They were safe.

The black mist was damn freaky. She didn't understand how the system worked. If she was in the middle of the haze, would it only transport part of her? If the Louers had tried to jump in, would only part of them make it? That thought shook her.

Still, they'd gotten away clean. Eric was here with her, Tammy was home and they were even bringing the Councilman back. There might be some skirmishing going on in Eric's dimension, but his people were perfectly capable of taking care of that problem now. Maybe she could finally go home. In truth, she wanted a hug from her mother. She couldn't believe how much she'd missed her.

The mist closed over her head.

"Thank heavens for that," she whispered.

"We're almost home now."

She closed her eyes and waited for the endless darkness to lighten. And waited. "Eric?"

"Another moment. The codex has stopped signaling."

His comforting tone of voice reassured her almost as much as his words. She breathed a sigh of relief. "Good, I was afraid something else had gone wrong."

"No. Everything's fine. Almost there."

The stiffness eased from her shoulders and her insides relaxed.

Just then two hands reached out and gave her a shove – hard. She lost her balance.

A shocked shriek escaped her.

ERIC REACHED OUT to grab her and yelled, "Storey? What's the matter?"

There was only silence.

And empty space.

CHAPTER 1

STOREY COULDN'T BREATHE. She bent over and gasped, desperately trying to force her chest open to let air in. The pressure was killing her. She didn't dare pass out in case she didn't wake up. She gulped air like a grounded fish, trying to take in as much oxygen as she could. With each breath her lungs expanded easier, faster. Finally, some of the tension slipped off her shoulders and her muscles eased slightly. She stretched her neck and willed the rest of the strain away.

Wherever she was, she lay surrounded in a dense gray fog. Not shadowy, like the Louers' world, but a completely empty type of gloominess. In spite of her attempts to stop it, shudders slid down her spine in a continuous tremor. What had happened?

Then she remembered. Of course. They'd almost made it home – her, Eric and the Councilman. Then she'd been pushed out of the portal.

Damn.

"Eric?" She called out tentatively. No answer. She called out louder. "Eric." Still nothing. She yelled his name next, and when only a deafening silence answered, she screamed at the top of her lungs. "Eric! Are you there?"

Silence. And not a normal silence. A total absence of…anything. Beyond weird.

What had she expected? Why was it she hadn't seen this coming? Not that she'd expected decent behavior from the man that had tried several times to have her killed, but to actually do the dirty work himself? That surprised her.

Stylus. She slapped her hands over the stylus, her pencil-like computer thingy. "Stylus, can you hear me?"

Yes.

"Oh thank you, God," she murmured. She closed her eyes. She wasn't alone. She could do this. With the stylus, she could do anything. Taking a deep breath, she let it go gustily, feeling her sense of optimism settle in. This was going to be okay. Feeling better, she asked, "Where are we?"

In-between.

Uh oh. Cautiously, she asked, "In-between what?"

Time and place.

She winced. That so didn't sound good. "What does that mean?"

It means we have no location.

No location? How could that be? She existed. Somewhere. Therefore there was a place. It was here. "Sooo..." she pressed. "How do we get out of this?"

We don't have that information.

Okay, so maybe this wasn't going to be so easy. She shook her head, more to clear the negativity than in denial. Although denial of the circumstances was there – by the bucket loads. "So not a good answer. We'll have to find the information. The longer we stay stuck like this, the harder it's going to be to get home."

So saying she took a deep breath and stood up. Her surroundings looked the same. She placed a hand out into the dense space in front of her, but there was nothing there. And that freaked her out more than she cared to admit. She crouched down and studied her feet. Her shoes were muddy and showing signs of damage after the past week. She'd have to find new ones soon. She winced. She was focusing on her shoes to avoid thinking of the fogginess around them, in front of them…under them. Yet she could see her feet – barely. She straightened. In the Louers' mine she'd at least been able to tap the hard surface of the floor and recognize that she'd come to the end of whatever drop she'd taken.

Here…she stretched out the tip of her right shoe and tried to tap the space in front of her left shoe. Her shoe went below her left foot. She gasped and pulled her foot back. She tried to stand on her right foot like she had been a minute earlier, only now there was nothing solid beneath it. Her foot slipped down until she caught herself and leaned all her weight onto her left shoe. Slowly she moved her foot around and tested the ground behind and in front of her. Only there was nothing there. Oh God. Oh God. *Oh God!*

She straightened and rested her right foot on her left foot and closed her eyes, trying to concentrate on her balance. Why wasn't she one of those agile gymnast-cheerleader types who could stand on one leg for hours? She breathed in and out, in and out. Somewhat balanced, but knowing she couldn't keep this up, she called out, "Stylus…a little help here."

When there was no response, she snapped, panicked, "Like now!"

Researching our database. Our records show some people going In-between.

She brightened. "That's good right? So how did these people get out?"

They only traveled to In-between as part of the journey to their end destination.

"In other words they didn't stop in…In-between. Which really means it doesn't apply to us," she said in exasperation. "Has anyone gotten stuck In-between that you know of?"

Of course. You.

She groaned and leaned her head back. Her left leg was starting to ache. She wasn't going to be able to do this much longer. She spread her arms out to stabilize her footing. "Anyone else?"

We are continuing to search the archives for more cases.

Damn. "So best guess? Am I going to continue to fall if I put my weight on my right foot?"

It's possible.

"Possible? Yeah. I know it's possible. But is it likely?" She'd woken up here. Surely she hadn't been sleeping standing up? What if she tried to sit? Did she dare? Did she have any choice?

Her left leg trembled. Beads of sweat formed on her upper lip and the headache she'd had since she woke, minor pounding until now, started to kick her butt. She groaned with the effort to continue standing on one foot.

You could fall. See where you stop.

Well, it couldn't be worse than this. Could it? Oh boy. She so didn't want to try it out and see. The fall could knock her out again too.

But…maybe she could sit very close to her feet? There had to be something there for her foot to stand on. She ignored the fact that there had to have been something for her right foot initially too. She hadn't heard anything drop away either. In fact, she could barely hear anything.

She took a deep breath and crouched down slowly, swearing at her unsteady movement. With her bum down as far as it could go, her arms wrapped tightly around her legs, she dropped her weight onto her backside, as close to the heel of her left foot as possible.

And sat down.

And fell backwards.

"STOREY! WHERE ARE you?" Eric spun around inside the confines of the portal. Only his father stood at his side. "What happened to her?" he asked him, a hard knot of suspicion forming in his gut.

His father opened his eyes wide, and held his hands out in innocence. Eric's suspicions solidified. "She must have fallen," his father said, his voice holding just that perfect mix of concern and confusion that he'd used so many times before.

And Eric knew. "You pushed her, didn't you?" He watched as surprised anger lit the depths of his father's gaze.

"I did not."

"Did too." Eric didn't care if he sounded like a two year old arguing the point. In truth he wanted to break down and cry. Things couldn't get much worse. For the first time, he didn't know what to do. Somehow, this seemed too big to deal with. How could he possibly help Storey now? And all because of his father.

His father snorted. "So what if I did. Good riddance I say. Her influence on you was nothing less than a disaster. You'd never have spoken so disrespectfully to me before." He stabbed the air with his index finger. "I blame her for the mess my life is in."

Eric glared at him, emotions welling up. He wanted to punch that smug look off his father's face. He balled his fist and pulled back his arm. A red wave of anger and a need to hit out at something overwhelmed him.

"Eric. Don't." Paxton's sharp voice caught Eric just as the power built in his upper arm. Eric stopped, frozen, a fierce welling of denial inside. This wasn't fair. His father deserved to get his ass kicked and Eric was just the one to do it.

"No! Not you." Paxton seemed to read his thoughts. "He will be punished. I heard what he said. We all did."

Releasing his breath in a heavy gust, Eric let his arm drop and turned to face his mentor and friend and a dozen of the council. He tried to school his features back into the non-emotional, calm expression his people were used to. He knew he didn't make it when Paxton took a small step forward, his hand outstretched toward him.

"He pushed her out of the portal," he cried out, anguish cracking his voice. "He pushed Storey out into the In-between. After she went and risked her own life...again...to rescue him."

The look of horror on the collective group of faces made him realize he wasn't alone in his shock and dismay. These people knew how final such a move was. How absolutely wrong it was. His people were peaceful, serene. Acts of violence were few and always shocking when they happened. But this...that their leader, even one that had been recently deposed...had done something so horrific to the visitor who'd saved them all...

If nothing else, it was satisfying to see the repugnance in their faces as they stared at his father.

Paxton ordered the Councilman to be taken under guard. Eric almost snorted at that. They didn't have much in the way of guards. At the rarely used underground dungeons, there might be a few on retainer, but they were hardly in prime condition.

"Throw him in the dungeon. That way he can't bribe anyone to let him out." Eric caught the outrage in his father's face. He turned. "Did you really think such an act would go unpunished? That you could return home a hero? That all your problems would go away if you could just get rid of Storey? Because I have to tell you, your problems are just starting. I for one will be asking for the death penalty."

At the shocked outcries from the others in the room, Eric strode as far away from his father as he could get and headed to Paxton's workbench. He had to focus on Storey. There was little information in the archives about In-between, the layer of nothing that existed between dimensions. Growing up he'd been fascinated by the early trials of portal travel. There'd been a few people who'd lost their lives in the development process. But he needed to go back and see if they'd ever rescued anyone who'd gotten lost In-between. Maybe there was a way to retrieve Storey. Or to help her find her way home.

Of course there was. Her stylus. Eric spun around searching for Paxton in the growing crowd. Where had all these people come from? He watched as more people rushed in to confirm the news. Had Storey really disappeared In-between? They'd talk until they had no more words to say, but that wasn't going to help Storey come home. He caught Paxton's eye, motioning him to come to his workspace.

"Everyone, let's move this discussion into the conference room." Paxton opened the double doors and motioned the crowd out of his space and into the large common room. "I need to speak with Eric first, then I will give you all an update as I know more. Please go in and get comfortable. We'll find a way to handle this mess."

"You'd better," someone called from the crowd.

"Storey needs our help. She helped us…"

"And the Councilman must pay for what he's done." Shouts and raised voices followed the group as it made its way into the larger room. Finally Paxton closed the main doors to the lab, locking them, and walked over to the workbench. "Now maybe we can have a few moments."

Eric strode over to the adjoining conference room door and shut it behind the last person moving through the lab to join the group mingling and talking loudly. This and the recent battle with the Louers had given them something to talk about for decades to come. Too bad most of it was at Storey's expense.

Paxton hurried toward him. "Now Eric, are you sure she's lost In-between?"

Eric ran a hand through his hair as he thought on what had happened. "She was in the portal with us. I could see her, then there was a small rush of wind, she shrieked and was gone. I searched the blackness, but you know you can't see very much at all during a transfer." He stopped for breath, and closed his eyes briefly. Would the echo of Storey's scream ever fade? He almost hoped not. He needed to keep her alive…until he could find a way to bring her back.

"We'll find a way to help her."

"We need to contact her stylus," Eric said. "See if it can communicate from In-between. If it can, we might be lucky and get a way out of this fast."

Paxton was ahead of him. He already had his stylus in his hand and an electronic tablet on the desk. In seconds his hand flowed over the screen. "My stylus is already checking. Our connection is growing every day." Paxton shook his head. "It can hear and anticipate my needs now."

Eric snorted. "After all this time? Unbelievable."

"I wished I'd known about their abilities earlier," Paxton admitted. "If it hadn't been for Storey…"

"Exactly. She's done so much for us," Eric muttered, peering down at the tablet. He couldn't read what Paxton's stylus was writing.

"Eric, back up. I can't see what I'm doing." The exasperation in Paxton's voice made Eric smile. He stepped back to give his friend room to work.

"It says it can hear the stylus, but there is great distance between them. Communication is splotchy."

Eric laughed with relief. Splotchy meant there was still some communication. "That sounds like Storey's vocabulary."

Paxton snorted. "Another of her influences."

There was no arguing with that comment. Storey had dropped into their world – literally – and they were forever changed. They needed to get her back safely to where she belonged. "But we can communicate. First off, let's make sure she's okay. I'd hate to think of her lying somewhere with a broken leg."

When there was no answer, Eric glanced at his mentor. The confusion on Paxton's face had him asking, "What's wrong?"

Paxton held out his hands, palms upwards. "There is *nothing* In-between. It's empty space. In theory she couldn't be hurt. There's nothing for her to have hit in the fall – unless she was carrying something. By that same logic, she should be unconscious from the pressure. The absence of atmosphere…I'd think." But he looked doubtful. He turned back to his stylus. "Let's find out what the stylus knows."

Not much was the answer that trickled in a few minutes later. The stylus said it was caught In-between, and had no information as to how to get home. It did confirm that Storey had been pushed from the portal just before the arrival at Paxton's lab and that she hadn't been physically hurt in the process. Just as Paxton started to ask another question, the communication was cut off.

Instead of feeling better, Eric paced, his mind full of more questions. Unfortunately, uninjured from the fall didn't mean she was *still* unhurt or if she'd suffered emotional or mental trauma.

Paxton seemed to think both were inevitable under the circumstances. But to Eric, Paxton was once again underestimating Storey. She was tough mentally. Stronger and more adept than any other female in Eric's acquaintance. But not even she could withstand atmospheric pressure issues like Paxton had described. If there was no atmosphere, she wouldn't be able to breathe either. And that meant it was all over. The stylus might not even know that yet. Eric shook his head at the puzzle. Did the stylus know when its owner was unconscious? Dead? It must, because the bond between stylus and owner would break. That was how the stylus had come to be Storey's in the first place – the bond between it and its previous owner had broken when the owner became ill. But if it was no longer bonded, could it still communicate with other styluses?

He shuddered. So many questions and no answers.

"Oh dear." Paxton murmured. "We need to be able to talk to her stylus."

That definitely understated the problem. Eric glanced at the monitor in front of him. "Why can't we access our archives here and see if there is anything helpful?"

"My stylus is looking for answers." Paxton rubbed his face. "We just have to be patient."

"Patient? Storey could be dying right now."

"Actually," Paxton took a deep breath, looked up at Eric, and in a low voice said, "It's more likely that she's already dead."

CHAPTER 2

S TOREY FELL INTO nothingness. Again. She twisted in
panic as her body went into freefall.

The thing was…she wasn't falling fast like a six story
drop. More like she was on a slow descent – almost as if
there was little to no gravity. And it appeared endless. What
the hell? No wind whistled past her ears, but her hair floated
gently upward from the force of changing altitude, not
streaming her like she'd expect.

And she should have stopped by now.

Suddenly she did.

"Ohhmph." She groaned at the shock as much as the
pain. Her face had smashed flat against a hard surface. An
invisible surface.

"Stylus what is going on?"

The humming in her head reassured her. That at least
was normal. She paused, her thoughts hiccupping on the
idea that speaking to a pencil was *normal* and having it
answer back was *normal* too. 'Cause neither would have been
something she'd have considered 'normal' any other time
except this last week. Lord her life had changed!

"Stylus, what am I lying on?"

Nothing.

"I can see that. How is this happening? It's like the rules
of normal reality don't exist here."

They don't. You aren't in the Louers', Torans' or your home world. In theory there might be no rules here. Or you might be able to create the rules you want.

That made her stop and think. The suggestion didn't feel wrong. As she considered the strangeness of what had happened to her since she'd arrived, it started to make even more sense. "Like stopping?" she questioned. "I was wondering about why I hadn't stopped falling, when all of a sudden, I stopped."

Maybe.

She closed her eyes, took a breath and said, "I'm falling."

Instantly her body dropped, leaving her stomach back where she'd been resting. *Shit.*

"Stop!"

She stopped, coming to another jarring slam against nothing. She laughed. How freaky cool was that? She rolled over and sat up. On nothing. "Now that's weird."

It would seem this reality answers to your thoughts, even instructions.

"And how cool is that?" Still, playing here for an hour or two was not the same thing as being stuck. But was she stuck? Could she get out the same way she'd stopped falling? She wouldn't know until she'd tried.

"I want to go home." Nothing. Then, getting all the way back to her reality might be a bit of a stretch. How about the one she'd left to arrive here? "I want to go back to Eric's dimension."

Try instructions not requests.

"Take me back to the Torans' dimension." Old habits rose to the surface and she added, "Please."

Nothing changed. "Okay, maybe there's a time delay?"

I don't think so. Everything is instant here.

She frowned. "Then what am I doing wrong?" She stood up and turned around. "Is anyone here? Can anyone hear me? Hello."

A faint echo sounded.

Hello.

She frowned. "An echo means something has to be here. Sound bounces off objects in order to create an echo. Right?" She couldn't remember much about the science behind the repeating sounds, but she was pretty sure they couldn't exist if they didn't have something to hit and rebound off. She vaguely remembered hearing an echo when she'd been screaming for Eric.

"Hello!" she shouted.

Hello.

There it was again, faint, but definitely an echo. Excited, she strode off in the direction of the sound. She kept her gaze in front of her so as to not look down at the endless nothingness beneath her feet. New reality or not, some fears needed to be kept submerged before she created them accidentally. "Stylus, is it possible that there could be people here? Like yet another reality? Maybe there's a whole new species of people who live in this In-between dimension. I mean, why not? I'm breathing and speaking. Thankfully I don't have to go to the bathroom or have an appetite right now, cause that's just not going to work out too well…but maybe there are others like me here." The concept brought a smile to her face and a lightness to her footsteps.

We don't believe so.

"But you don't know – do you? And if you don't know, you can only guess." She laughed. "This is new for both of us. Not just me."

Since meeting you, there has been much new for both of us.

She stopped, considered the stylus's words and nodded. "True enough. Well, together we can find whatever the sounds are bouncing off of. Maybe that will lead us to a way out."

Or lead you further from your point of entry.

Ah shit. She hadn't thought of that. She spun around and looked back the way she'd come. Of course, she could see exactly…nothing.

And she'd lost track of how long she'd been travelling. "Do you think I need to keep track of where I landed?" She chewed on her bottom lip, worrying away on that new concern and wishing she'd thought of it earlier. "Did you keep track of it?"

We have noted the coordinates of your entrance point to this dimension and your exit point from the Toran dimension.

She brightened. "So we can go back there at any time, right?"

In theory, yes. However as our knowledge doesn't cover this instance, we can't confirm that.

She pondered that. "I think you should keep track of every step I take here. On all levels. Because we fell a long way in that first drop. Add the other couple of smaller falls and the vertical distance could be huge. It might be hard to get back up there."

You should be able to think yourself back there.

She nodded. Theoretically that might be possible, in reality, well, that remained to be seen. Should they try to regain their same starting position? But she'd tried that back when she'd first entered the Louers' dimension. She'd ended up in a whole different location.

And if that happened here, she'd lose track of where the echo had come from. She spun around only to realize she wasn't at all sure she was facing the right direction anymore. Damn it.

She stood for a moment, hands on her hips and studied the thick endless fog around her. "Hello?"

No echo. Although there appeared to be something. She turned slightly and called out louder, "Hello."

No echo. Maybe it wasn't an echo? She turned to the other side and yelled, "Hello."

Hello.

And damn it. That didn't sound the same at all.

Still, she didn't have much choice but to go forward and find out.

"HOW IS IT that we have no idea how to help Storey?" Eric refused to contemplate that she was dead. She'd find a way to survive. She was unlike anyone else he'd ever known. And she'd get out of this mess just like she'd gotten out of any number of her other chaotic disasters.

She had to. Anything less was unthinkable.

Paxton opened his mouth…hesitated and closed it again. Then he took a deep breath and said, "I don't think she's alive."

"I do." Eric was stalwart in his stance. "There's no way she's not." He glared down at the stylus in Paxton's hand. "Ask it more questions. There has to be a way to track her."

"And what good will that do?" Paxton stared at him, concern growing in his gaze. "You can't go in after her. That's not possible."

Eric studied him. "It is you know. If we can track her on this side, I can set the coordinates, port to where she is, then port home again."

But Paxton was shaking his head. Tufts of hair flying in all directions. "No. No. That's not possible. You could be lost in there with her."

"And I could get her back again. We owe it to her. I owe it to her. It's my father who sent her there."

"We can't lose you, too. No." Paxton lifted both hands to his head and tugged on the ends of his hair. "No. You can't go after her."

"Then find a way to leave breadcrumbs for her to follow so she can get out on her own."

Paxton brightened. Eric could only imagine at what he was thinking. His mentor had been impressed with Storey, but he'd sacrifice her in a heartbeat if it meant keeping Eric safe. Unlike his own father, Paxton cared.

But now Eric had to get Paxton to care about Storey. Enough to help her to get out. And this could be the way. Have him help Storey in order to keep Eric safe. "Let's ask the stylus to track her?"

Paxton sniffed. "I already have."

Eric rolled his eyes. But not so the older man could see. "And?"

"It's trying to contact Storey's stylus. The communication is getting worse."

"Could she be moving further away?"

"Or she's…fading." Paxton shot him a quick look. Eric glared back at him. "But we won't go there yet."

Paxton refocused on his paper and the stylus in his hand, busy writing down a message. "The stylus has a location for Storey."

Eric grinned. "Good. I knew this could work."

"But…" Paxton held up a cautioning hand. "The location is changing."

"Of course it is." She wasn't dead. Relief washed over him. He'd been right. "She's going to be moving around. Trying to come back."

"Maybe, but she needs to be back at the same point she arrived at in order to leave. Otherwise time will have changed."

"Oh, shit." Not that whole time thing again. Last time they'd messed with time, things had gone from bad to worse before they could get back where they belonged.

Paxton spun around and stared at him in shock.

Eric shook his head. "Sorry. I don't mean to swear. It's Storey's influence, I know. I'll stop."

Paxton thrust his nose up at an amazing altitude even for him. Then his hand jerked on the paper as the stylus started to move.

"Her stylus has the coordinates of where they landed. It says Storey can see nothing. It's like being in thick fog. The place is empty. She heard an echo so is looking to locate the reason. The stylus is tracking her movements."

Eric laughed. "That's Storey. She's off exploring."

"It's dangerous." Paxton glared. "She should have stayed put."

Paxton didn't understand. Eric did. He admired Storey's courage. Her sense of making life happen instead of standing by and watching it happen. He needed to do more of the same. He should go over and help her. He frowned, remembering something else Paxton had said. "There were other men lost In-between, you said. Is there any chance they could still be alive?"

The speed with which Paxton spun around stunned Eric. He backed up a step. "Whoa. I was just asking."

Paxton stared, his thoughts obviously engaged elsewhere.

"Paxton? Is that possible?"

He pursed his lips, then shook his head regretfully. "No. It's been much too long."

"What's been too long?" Eric studied the emotions rippling across his friend's face. "Did you know someone who was lost?"

"There have been very few people lost there. Mostly in the beginning when portal travelling was being worked out. Most died from being half in and half out when the transfer completed. Since then, only one, no two, have been lost completely In-between. One because he had a heart attack while travelling and fell out of the portal. We're pretty sure he was dead first though. And then there was a young man whose foolish behavior sent him through the portal into the In-between during travel."

Eric winced. Not a great way to die. Paxton looked as if he wanted to say more, but he closed his mouth, his lips pressed firmly together.

"What aren't you telling me?"

Paxton sighed, then broke down. "That young man has been In-between for over a century and a half." He paused, swallowed loudly and added, "He was my younger brother."

"Your brother?" Eric stared at him. "I didn't know you had one. That must have been terrible." He shook his head. Unbelievable. "Have you tried to get him back?"

"He was a young man at the time, but always acting the fool. We were a group of six, and he was trying to impress the ladies and tripped and fell In-between." Paxton frowned, his eyes losing focus as if gazing back into the years past. "We've never had a way to go in and find him. Or find what was left of him."

He picked up the stylus that he'd laid down on the tablet. "If only I'd known about this back then. But I'd just bonded with it. We were still getting to know each other. It was all so new. And I was so full of myself and my new status." He shook his head. "And our knowledge was so limited."

"Maybe we can track your brother down. At least find his remains and bring him home."

Paxton looked hopeful for a short moment, then shook his head. "No. There's no way to know where he went over. He could be anywhere and after so long, he must be dead. I can't imagine there is food or water there." He sighed heavily, as if he was letting go of a long held wish. "No, death should have come immediately and if not, then within days to a week at the most."

Eric wasn't so sure of that. If there was anything over there to find, Storey would be the one to find it.

CHAPTER 3

"HELLO?" STOREY CALLED out, her head cocked to hear the echo. There it was, faint, but solid. She walked quickly toward it. As quickly as she dared. In the dense nothingness, she didn't dare look up or down. She focused on the sound, her hands out in front, and tried to keep a steady course forward. In her mind, she held to the thought of finding whatever created the echo.

She didn't understand how this place worked and with the stylus still not up to full strength… Were her messages to Paxton and Eric even getting through? She hadn't heard anything in response. And that wasn't good. She was running out of options. She had to find a way to boost the Stylus's power. Fast.

And she had to figure out if there was anything useful in this In-between dimension to make that happen. She called out again, and again, each time getting closer to the source of the echo. She felt like a fool, but there was nothing new in that. She'd never have tried to go through the portal in her bedroom floor if she'd been worried about what other people thought of her. She knew she was 'different.' Tough. Who said different was bad?

She dropped her arms and picked up the pace to sprint forward and smacked into…something…hard.

"Oomph." Storey groaned as she stumbled backwards,

tried to regain her balance and fell on her butt. She shook her head and looked up.

And looked again.

"Hello," she said cautiously. There appeared to be a person in front of her. A man. But he was tilting forward several feet in front of her. In fact he was leaning so far forward she didn't understand what kept him upright. Then remembered where she was.

The fog was so dense, she could barely see his features. She edged forward and studied him closely, noting his Toran style pants and shirt, his brown hair and oddly preserved-looking features. He couldn't be more than mid-twenties, but there was something off to his face, as if it were weathered, like an antique. He slowly shook his head, as if waking from a deep sleep.

Yet he didn't straighten. He opened his eyes, blinked several times, then closed them as if to snooze off again.

She was both relieved to see someone here and yet at the same time…discomfited at his oddness. Even after all she'd seen. Still, having another person to talk to, to bounce ideas off of, to show her how to manage this new dimension was huge. Her breath gusted out and her shoulders relaxed. She was not alone.

"Hello," she repeated quietly, not sure what else to do, but not wanting to freak him out.

His eyes flew open and he twisted his head enough to see her. Now he looked really odd because he still leaned so far forward.

Storey walked in front of him, hoping he'd straighten. And he did, slightly.

"W…who…are you?" he asked, his voice a whisper of sound in the air.

"I'm Storey Dalton. I just arrived here." She grimaced. She sounded like a damn tourist. She took a deep breath. "Who are you, and how long have you been here?"

He blinked, yet the rest of him remained eerily still.

Now this was going to get irritating. Storey hadn't realized how much of a get up and go person she really was until she'd started crossing dimensions. And how different she was from others. And not only her own people. The Torans with their endless discussions, the Louers with their communication system that didn't include her and now this brain fogged sleeper. Nothing moved as quickly as she'd like.

"Hello? Are you in there?" She leaned closer, gazing into his eyes. She was hoping to see some kind of light come on. A sign of comprehension – of knowledge that he needed to wake up – and proof that was going to happen.

She got another blink.

So not helpful. She reached out a tentative hand and watched as his eyes tracked her movement. Talk about creepy. She gently squeezed his shoulder, a little surprised to find him solid. She'd begun to wonder if he was real or as insubstantial as the rest of this world.

"Stylus, who is this person. And what's wrong with him. He appears to be barely conscious."

He should be unconscious.

"Why? I'm not?"

He's been here much too long to remain conscious.

"Well he might have been unconscious before, but I did run into him. Hard. Could that have woken him up?" She bent to look into the man's face again. "Sorry about that by the way." He blinked. She grimaced. "Stylus, I think he hears me and sees me, but I'm not sure he's doing much comprehending."

It may take him time to come around. He could have been here for centuries. We have found only two men recorded to having fallen In-between in the last quarter millennia.

She straightened. "Centuries," she repeated, hating the tremor that wavered through her voice. Hell, her whole body was starting to quake. "Surely that's not possible. How could he survive here all that time? His body needs food and water…doesn't it?"

This is not a physical reality. Time does not exist here.

Time. She was really starting to hate that element. It kept screwing up her world.

But in fact, you are the one that keeps…screwing…with time.

She grinned. "Hey stylus, you're really loosening up. Good on you."

You have introduced new words and language patterns. We are attempting to integrate these into our knowledge base.

She had to laugh. "Not sure that's a good idea, but hey, you will always remember my influence on your world this way. Nice to know I'll be remembered."

You will always be remembered.

Her thoughts turned melancholy. Would she? If she stayed in here? Eric would mourn her, Paxton would put her into the archives and the Councilman would cheer. Her mother could already be past the worst stage of grief. For all she knew, her old life was gone – maybe had never even existed in the first place if she'd truly twisted up time like it appeared she had. In which case, she most likely would never have been born. And if that wasn't a mind-bender to consider.

She so had to go back and fix that.

But first she had to fix this mess. She couldn't help but

feel like it was all getting to be too much. She really wanted to just go home. Something she'd been trying to do since…well, forever.

This man had to know something. Therefore he was just going to have to wake up enough to share it. To that end, she reached over and gave him a hard slap on the shoulder. "Wake up. I need to know how to get out of here."

He blinked.

Was he in there? Conscious? Normal? She peered at him, wondering. Maybe he had brain damage. That fear jumped inside and wouldn't let go. She closed her eyes and prayed for patience. She opened them and tried again. "Please, tell me how to escape from here."

His mouth opened and his voice, rusty from disuse, whispered, "There is no escape."

ERIC RETURNED TO his home and packed. He didn't know what exactly he might need, but was determined to make sure he had as much in the way of supplies as possible. Storey could get into trouble like no one he'd ever known. But she always got out of it. It's just sometimes she needed a little help. He loaded a pack with emergency food rations, water, clothes and first aid supplies.

This was one of those times. He pulled the codin clip from his belt and connected it to his pack, then sucked the pack into its envelope form. Storey loved this technology. It let him shrink wrap almost any household item down to a packet the size of a small envelope without damaging the contents. Just thinking about Storey made him remember something else. He tucked the pack away in his back pocket, then pulled out an empty one. Storey might need extra paper. Not something he had here. He returned to Paxton's lab to find his mentor at the workbench. "Any news before I leave?"

Paxton's back stiffened. "Leave?"

"Paxton, I have to try and rescue her. She would do the same for me. She *has done* just that. I can't sit by now when she's trapped In-between."

The older man's face grayed and although already sitting, he seemed to shrink into himself. "I know," he whispered. "I'd hoped I could make you see reason but…"

"I may not need to if we can help her rescue herself." Eric motioned to his table full of stuff. "But I'm preparing to go just in case."

He eyed the stack of codexes. Navigation was an inherent skill for him. Except in the In-between nothing might work – tools or instinct. The last thing he wanted was to get over there and wish he had brought more equipment. He added several to his pocket. He precoded them to save time.

"Eric, look here…" Paxton stood up and pointed to the big monitor in front. He had some kind of blank screen set up with only lights flashing to show anything existed on it. "The top marker is the location Storey entered In-between, according to the coordinates given by her stylus. It has kept a running guide of her travels. As you can see, she's all over the place." The screen rotated to show Storey's progress from various points of view, eventually morphing into a three dimensional picture.

Eric walked closer. "I don't understand. Why are some of these higher? Is this a map?"

Paxton's head bobbed. "That's the issue. She's not moving north or south *only*, she's also moving up and down. The system is tracking the changes in her altitude."

"Are there mountains there?" Eric didn't understand. Yet even as he watched, the signal moved again. This time slightly higher. He tapped the screen. "So you are saying that this little jag up in her pathway is actually an altitude change and not a few steps to the north?"

"Exactly. On the whole she is moving toward the north. But you could walk for hours following her tracks and never see her because she could be above you or below, out of your line of sight. And the fog is likely all encompassing. You wouldn't see her until you hit her."

That just reminded Eric of finding Storey in the Louers' dimension. His codex had locked onto hers and he'd tracked her all the way through the Louers' housing. In fact, she'd jumped him out of the darkness as her stylus had told her he was there already. He pointed that out to Paxton.

"Yes, but there's no guarantee that the codex will function there." Paxton replied. "If north isn't north and gravity is nonexistent, all the machinery will be off too."

Yeah, he got that. He stared down at his codex. The arm band covered the bulk of his forearm. An essential tool of his work and lifestyle. And he'd been forced to use the codex in so many ways lately. For travelling, communication, even tracking. He hated knowing that it might not be there for him In-between. "Can we do anything to make my codex more adaptable? Boost it in some way. Give it an alternative navigational system? Alternate power? Something else?"

Paxton stared at him, his brows narrowed in concentration. He stood suddenly and walked to his workbench on the side. "We can boost the tracking system. That will help us to know where you are at all times."

Eric wasn't sure that would help. It would drive Paxton nuts to be able to track Eric, but not know how to bring him home. "What about the stylus? Does it have any suggestions on how to adapt or strengthen the codex?"

Paxton shrugged, but picked up the stylus and his tablet. The stylus immediately started to write. Paxton read the message out loud. "We didn't always have portal travel. In the beginning, to establish the pathways, we had to learn how to go In-between."

In-between? Paxton and Eric stared at each other. "I'm sorry. Did you say you had to go In-between to make the portal travel system work?"

The stylus started writing. *That's how it works. You go between time-space reality to land in a new place. We made many mistakes early on. But it was one of us who created this process.*

"One of you?" Eric stared at the stylus. He still couldn't get over the fact that there were souls inside the tool.

One of us not in here.

And wished, not for the first time, that they'd speak clearer and with less riddles. "If not one of you in there, then who?"

He who exists in the broken one. He is much revered by us all. He had been lost to us until Storey saved him.

Storey again. She just kept gaining admirers. Eric turned to Paxton. "Where are they? The styluses that Storey rescued," he explained at Paxton's blank look. "She gave them to you for safe keeping."

Paxton was already up off his chair and racing to the far side of the room. He unlocked a cupboard and removed a large box. Carefully he placed it down on his desk and opened it. There inside, on a purple cushion, rested the styluses Storey had brought back from the Louers' dimension.

Paxton grabbed up his tablet and stylus, quickly asking which of the styluses could help.

Before the stylus could give instructions, Eric had rummaged through and found the thick broken one. It looked similar to the others, but older, more crude in design. Like an early prototype. "Got it."

Yes that one.

Eric looked down at the stylus in Paxton's hand. "How did it know which one I was holding?"

Paxton's hand jerked. *We can see. And feel. As you touched the others, we registered the change in temperature. You hold the correct one.*

See? The stylus could see. See what? Everything? The more he learned, the more bizarre these tools became. Seeing, however, could be very helpful in finding Storey.

"How can we wake this broken stylus up?"

It is damaged. He is too weak.

"No. See, I'm not going to accept that. He has information that Storey needs to escape her prison. As she saved him, he needs to save her."

The air filled with a high level buzz that had Eric spinning around in panic. It was too reminiscent of the Louers' attack on Eric's world, before Storey created a whole new world for the Louers.

Even Paxton seemed to shake nervously. "It's the stylus," he exclaimed. He dropped the tool on the tablet and backed away. "Maybe it's going to blow up. Maybe we did something to it. Broke it somehow?"

Eric took a step closer and the buzz intensified. He held out the broken stylus and again the sound intensified. "I think…they are talking to each other."

Paxton rushed forward. "Why so loud? They've never

done that before."

"Because this one is broken and…old." At least that was the best answer Eric could come up with. He looked at Paxton and shrugged. "This one might be damaged, but that doesn't mean his information isn't good."

"Then it should be in the database and archived with the rest of the information. It's unacceptable that one stylus should still contain sole ownership of any information." Paxton looked so affronted at the breach in protocol that Eric had to laugh.

"You might want to consider that it might be so old that it was created *before* the rules became protocol. They might have been just guidelines back then. Also consider that it might have been broken before the information could be sent to the archives."

"Harrumph," Paxton said. He glared at the two styluses. "How long is this noise going to keep up?"

Even as he finished speaking the buzz in the air eased down several decibels. "Makes you wonder if they heard your complaint and decided to tone it down a bit."

"They are instruments. Not reasoning beings," Paxton said testily.

Eric slid a sideways glance over at his mentor. Even with all he'd learned about his stylus, Paxton still didn't get it. There were people inside. Real souls. Not living breathing souls as in walking, talking Torans, but real, functioning, thinking souls without a body. But Eric himself might not have understood if it hadn't been for Storey and the way she'd communicated with her stylus. The damn thing *could* read her mind at this point. And apparently, she'd be able to read its thoughts soon, too. And if that didn't blow away all their beliefs about a stylus being only an instrument, what would?

"Could Storey communicate with the broken one?"

"How could she? She's not bonded to it."

Eric wondered about that. Storey, he knew, would have something to say about that kind of narrow thinking. Paxton just didn't know what few limitations she'd found with her own stylus. If this stylus had information they needed…

Taking a chance, he slipped the broken stylus into his pocket.

CHAPTER 4

"THERE HAS TO be something here." Even the sound of Storey's own voice failed to reassure her. She was in deep shit. In the grim fog surrounding her, everything was amplified. Including her fear. Damn. She stopped, closed her eyes and took a deep, calming breath. She had to stay in control. She had to stay composed. She didn't dare let fear take over. She'd end up as mindless jelly.

This could be the end of everything, but she didn't dare focus on that. Especially here. She might create that end before she understood what she'd done. Then she'd never get back to Eric's world. She'd never make it home. She'd never see her mother again. Or fix the mess she'd left behind. That so couldn't happen. How could her life be cut short before she'd done what she needed to do? She had yet to live. Had yet to love. Had yet to be loved.

There's no way she could die.

She refused.

And laughed. If insisting something could make it so, then she had this place beat. She wasn't going to knock the value of positive thinking. She'd had too much of it drilled into her from her mom, who believed anything could happen if a person wanted it badly enough. Right now, Storey desperately wanted her mother to be right.

'Cause positive thinking was all that she appeared to

have available to her.

Damn.

"Stylus, is there any way to draw in the air – versus on paper like I normally do – and have you take us out of here?"

No.

"Well then, let's draw on my jeans again. Although I don't think I can port through those – or could I?" She looked down at her already doodle-covered jeans, then pulled her shirt up. She didn't remember writing on her skin last time, but this time she'd do it in a heartbeat if it meant getting the hell out of here. She stared at the glowing gold pattern on her skin. Honor marks, Paxton had called them.

In the darkness, they were a bright beacon. If anyone were looking for her.

It's not the surface. It's the medium, the atmosphere, that is the problem. I can't move us through this to another dimension.

Storey shook her head. At least she could just talk to her stylus. Saved on writing surfaces. "See that doesn't make sense. We drew portals from the Louers' dimension to my dimension. Sure, we ended up back in time then, but we still managed to travel."

I don't have the coordinates.

Storey stopped. "Yes you do. You have the coordinates for Eric's place, my homeland and even the Louers' world. Take us to anyone of those."

I can't. I don't have the coordinates of where we are here.

"But you said that you were going to keep track of the coordinates of where we landed before I started to move to where I thought I heard the echo."

Yes, I have the location of where we landed, but we don't have anything to measure those against in this dimension. I have to have a map of this dimension in order to calculate a way out of it. A point of origin. To move anywhere, I need to know the point we are starting from.

"Then get it from Paxton!" She was beside herself with excitement. They could do this. They would do this.

Communication is faulty. And there is no guarantee that they will have this location. No one has been here before.

She sighed and rubbed her eyebrows. "You mean no one has returned from here. So what do we need to do to improve the communication?"

An odd hum filled the air. She grinned. A welcome sound. It meant the stylus was thinking about a solution.

The sound cut off.

We need more power. This place is difficult, more complicated.

"Fine. How do we get more power?"

More of us. We are damaged.

She rolled her eyes. She'd heard that a lot lately. "And how do you expect us to do that?"

"We don't."

"Can Paxton help?"

No. Communication is faulty.

She sighed and pinched the bridge of her nose. Okay. Back to the same problem.

The faint cough at her side made her look up. Right – the odd guy she'd found. "Hey, you don't have any idea how to increase our power here, do you?"

He stared at her, a blank look in his eyes. As if finally understanding she was serious, he shook his head. Even that motion appeared to pain him. It was like his body hadn't moved in many years. And she didn't know how that could be.

"Stylus, can we do anything to help ourselves from this

side?" The stylus was quiet. Damn it. Storey wanted to pound something but in this foggy land of nothing, there was nothing to pound.

She turned to the almost asleep-on-his-feet man. "Are there others here?"

She had to nudge him and repeat the questions. He shook his head and in a voice barely above a whispers, said, "No. Not since a long time."

She jumped on that. "Since a long time? What does that mean? Are there other people lost here?"

He gave a slight shake of his head. "I don't know. I never saw anyone."

"Let's find out. If there is someone here, maybe they can help."

If they had a way out, they would have left.

Storey wasn't sure when the stylus had started to get a personality, but this dimension appeared to bring it to the surface. "But they didn't have you."

The hum started again. Storey glanced over at the man. He appeared to be asleep again. It was odd. Had he slept through the last century? Did he have food or water? And if he did, that meant body functions. Still, there appeared to have been little to no aging in all the decades or centuries that he'd been stuck here. Had time stopped for him? And if so, what would happen to him when it started again?

Stylus, she asked mentally. *Is he okay? If he's been here all these years, can he survive in the Torans' world now?*

He's been comatose for all this time.

Right. Was that good or bad?

Does that mean we can take him back or we can't? I don't want him to die when we get home, but... She chewed on her bottom lip. This was a new concern. Originally, all she'd wanted was to get home. Now she wanted take this poor man with her and…she was very much afraid he couldn't go back. That was a horrible concept…and one she had to question in her own case.

We believe he will die.

Will he? She glanced over at the sleeping man. *Are you sure?*

Yes. And if you stay here, it will be your fate too.

ERIC FINISHED PACKING, doubled checked that the broken stylus was safe, then tucked it away in his inside jacket pocket. He didn't mention it to Paxton. The scientist was protective of all the styluses, and Eric didn't want him to refuse to let it go.

Still, if there was any chance this one had information for Storey, then all the more reason to bring it to her. Just because Paxton said she couldn't access the information, didn't mean that was fact. As he was quickly learning, Storey knew a lot more about some stuff than most Torans.

A fact that would irritate them all. Especially his father.

"While I'm gone, you'll make sure to keep my father locked up, right?" When an answer wasn't immediately forthcoming, Eric spun around, "Right?"

Paxton nodded. "Yes. Still, I wish you wouldn't go."

"I know." But that wouldn't stop Eric. "So help me minimize the danger."

Paxton held out a weird instrument. "Just in case there are no landmarks or sky to work with, I'm going to give you a different type of tracker." He stood up and walked over to his workbench. He opened a drawer on the left side. Inside the drawer was another locked box. Eric leaned over. He'd never seen this box.

Paxton opened the box and pulled out a small, pill-like object. "Here. Swallow this."

Eric stared down at the thing. His stomach heaved. He didn't like the sound of this at all. "Do I have to? I can't imagine what it could do in there."

"This tracker will flush out of your system in a few days. In the meantime it will track your body heat in case we lose communications."

"But you already can track me. Look…" He pointed at Storey's moving pathway. "Track me like her."

"I'm tracking her stylus, not her." Paxton waited patiently.

Eric looked from the pill to his mentor and back again. "Fine. But I don't like it."

"You never did like to take your medicine, did you?"

Eric rolled his eyes at the mention of his childhood behavior and tossed the pill into his mouth. With difficulty he swallowed it dry.

"Good. Now we'll set it up and it should go live in a few minutes." He turned back to his monitors, his fingers busy on the keyboard. "Do you have everything you might need?"

"Paper? Something for Storey to write on if need be?"

Paxton found a spare tablet in a different drawer by his knees. He held it out.

"The only thing is these are small. She has these huge paper sheets that work well. And being electronic – will it even work over there?" Eric stared down at the tablet. He didn't think it would work to jump through the same way as the many paper portals Storey had drawn.

"We gave up paper decades ago," Paxton said testily.

"And that's why I was wondering if I should port to Storey's bedroom and grab more of her sketchbooks. Her closet has several of them." Storey'd had everything she needed for the last trip to the Louers' dimension, and as far as he remembered, she'd still had her travelling pouch during that last jump with his father. But…that didn't mean she still had it. What if she'd lost her pouch in her fall? According to what he'd learned so far, that could mean the pack was there, but just out of sight.

Besides, the more supplies the better.

The more he considered it, the better he like the idea. He might be able to scoop up some of her never ending stash of granola bars, too.

"I don't like all this traffic. You know it creates tunnels between dimensions when we do too much of it. That's why visits to her dimension are so carefully regulated."

"I understand that. But we have to do what we can to make sure that we have all options covered. If her paper can create a portal to get us out – like she created to allow us to rescue my father – then we should have more in *this* situation." Maybe the gentle reminder of how many times Storey had used paper to save their lives would help nudge Paxton. Eric didn't know if cross-dimension travel was an issue based in reality or just another of Paxton's unfounded worries.

How could anyone know?

"Then make it quick. In and out. Let no one see you and get back here immediately. Time is running out. If you're going to try and find Storey, I think you need to go there as soon as possible. The damage to her system, providing she's even alive, will increase by the hour."

Crap. "I didn't need to hear that," Eric muttered. "I'm going to run. Back within the hour."

CHAPTER 5

STOREY TOOK ANOTHER look at the man leaning at the impossible angle. If she'd found one person, would she find more if she stayed here longer? And how? She couldn't help but think it was only dumb luck that had brought her to this man in the first place. He still hadn't given her his name. She'd feel better talking to him if she knew what to call him.

She leaned across and nudged his shoulder. Then nudged it again – harder.

He blinked at her. Damn that was irritating. "Hey, remember me? What is your name?" She spoke clearly and slowly. Maybe it would help him understand.

"Dillon." He frowned as if surprised by his answer. "I think."

"Dillon. Good. That's a good start. How long have you been here, Dillon?"

His frown deepened. "I…don't know."

"Right. That probably wasn't the best question to ask you as time doesn't seem to matter here. Okay, Dillon, do you have any family back home that might be missing you?"

She winced. Probably not a good question either. But she needed to find out something about him. Just in case they could find a way to keep him alive. She refused to entertain the concept of failure in this case. Any information she could find would help Paxton sort this out. And let Dillon's family know what had happened to him.

"Brother," he said faintly, closing his eyes and swaying as if the effort had taxed him.

Excellent. His brain was functioning. "Good. You have a brother. He might be still alive too. What's his name?"

Dillon looked at her in confusion. Not that she'd seen many other expressions from him yet. She did get the impression she was disturbing his sleep. Something he was falling back into every time she stopped talking to him. So she kept talking. "Dillon?" she sharpened her voice this time.

He straightened ever so slightly. But it helped. His face had a familiar look to it. But, then, the Torans looked like humans.

"Yes?"

"You have a brother," she prompted, trying to hold in her exasperation. "What is his name?"

"Paxton."

"Paxton! Your brother is Paxton?" What were the odds? She shook her head. "Wait there must be more than one man with that name in your world. Hell, we have thousands of guys named Eric in mine. It must be a different man." But wouldn't it be cool if it was the Paxton she knew? She'd love to reunite the brothers.

If this one survived the trip. She wasn't even sure he could walk. What would happen to his body in a normal dimension? Whatever 'normal' meant. Space travel in her world apparently did horrible things to the human body. Something to do with radiation and no gravity. She couldn't imagine the gravity issue being any better on the body here.

"Stylus, we can't leave him behind. That's so not going to happen."

Dillon raised his head slightly. "Leave? There is no way to leave." His face crumpled. "I've been here for so long."

"What about water and food? Have you eaten anything in all these years?"

Dillon's eyes widened. "No. Sleep. I've been asleep. Until you came." He straightened a little more and looked around. "I remember hoping, waiting for rescue. When it didn't come, I slept. Until now."

"Until now? Really?" So not good. "Stylus, is that possible?"

In a comatose state similar to an animal in hibernation, yes, I believe so.

"Yes, but even a bear wakes up and comes out of his home when he's hungry. Dillon's system shut down. Completely."

Not completely. He is waking up. Slowly. If his body had shut down, he'd be dead. But there will be more problems as his body comes back to a more normal state.

"And is that going to mean his bodily needs are going to wake up too? I doubt I have enough food and water for a century long appetite." She'd reverted to speaking to the stylus out loud instead of in her mind. The sound of her voice was more appealing than the smothering silence. The normalcy of hearing her own voice somehow added balance to yet another bizarre situation.

"Stylus…I was thinking. Can't we just go back in time to before I was pushed out of the portal?"

They'd gone back in time accidentally before, but they'd survived that trip and she had no doubt that she'd survive it again. Staying here didn't look very survivable – not if Dillon was anything to go by.

No. I don't believe so.

"But that's not the same thing as no. Is it?" she prodded.

No. As the air here is different, I can't say that anything will work. We have no archival information of this.

"You guys did time travel before, right? Because you helped us last time."

But you didn't use my help to go back in time. I helped you find a way forward.

Splitting hairs as far as she was concerned. Time travel was time travel. Although technically the stylus was correct – again. That didn't mean it was *always* correct.

She sat down in front of Dillon. "I should have some paper and rations. I think." She pulled out the shrunken pack Eric had made for her in triumph. "And I have this." She waved it around. Eric should have the other pack – maybe. "Stylus can you open this?"

Yes.

"Good. Um…how? What do I need to do?"

Even as the last words tripped off her lips, a weird set of musical notes that sounded familiar rang out. And how the stylus could do that without speakers she didn't know. She laughed. "That's perfect. How come you don't play music to lighten the air?"

How can music lighten the air?

Storey shook her head. "It's a figure of speech. Music makes people feel good. It lightens their moods, their souls. Makes people happy."

Interesting.

She stared at it. "That's all you have to say? It seems much of your education is missing."

Education? We have had no education. We are Louers. Slaves. We received no education.

That whole ugly history thing again. She sympathized,

but this was so not the time. "Back to the problem then. I have a piece of paper. Why not just draw a portal back to Paxton's lab?"

We don't have a location for where we are at.

She pursed her lips, finally starting to understand there were limitations to the stylus. She hadn't come up against them before, because she hadn't really understood how the stylus had done what it did. Now she realized it had need of certain information to follow through on some of her requirements and for the first time they were both in new territory and neither knew what to do.

"What if we try it anyway?"

She pulled out an old portal she'd stashed in the pack a long time ago. Unfolding it, she found it led to Paxton's lab. She grinned and stood up. She placed the portal on the ground and reached out a hand to Dillon. "Dillon, step on this paper, please."

He blinked. He reached out a hand. Grabbed hers and stepped on the paper.

ERIC STUDIED THE trees and bushes of Storey's world as the black mist of the portal dissipated. It looked the same as the first time he'd ventured here. The size of the trees and the season all appeared to fit. But with the time shifts and new dimensions being created – he no longer trusted what stood before his own eyes. And how sad was that.

Before meeting Storey, life had been simple and complete…and boring. Now he felt so energized and alive. In ways he'd never experienced before and could hardly explain. But life thrummed through his veins now. Sure, so did worry and fear, but that was better than ennui.

And the weird thing was, he hadn't realized how lacking his previous life really had been. Ignorance really was bliss. He'd read that saying in the archives and had to admit there was some truth to it.

He walked the path to Storey's house, keeping a wary eye out. He should be in the right dimension and the right time frame, but as Storey had messed with things here, twisted time as the stylus had put it, he didn't know what to expect each time he came.

That brought back memories of Tammy, the little Louer child they'd rescued from her old home dimension. He grinned at the memory of her insatiable appetite. And her scream. He shuddered. That was very forgettable. At least he wished it were.

The house loomed ahead of him. He walked cautiously around to the front to see if any of the metal boxes Storey called cars were there. None. His breath gusted out in relief. That didn't mean no one was home, just meant there were likely less people at home. He stepped back into the trees and punched the coordinates for Storey's bedroom into his codex. He could have done it this way from the beginning, but the thought of porting into a stranger's bedroom while they were there made him cringe. With Storey having shifted time, there was no guarantee that he was in the same time as when Storey had lived here. The less he had to explain the better. And according to Storey, he should avoid capture at all costs. Something about not having the right identification or history. He shrugged. The black mist rose up around his shoulders, quickly blocking out the world around him. When it cleared he smiled. This was still Storey's bedroom.

The same bed, pictures on the wall, sketchbooks and paper tossed haphazardly around the room. So much of her personality permeated the room it made him smile. And then he froze. This was exactly like the first time he'd seen Storey's room. When only her mother lived with her here.

What had happened to the time twist where Storey's life had shifted, creating an alternate form of the reality she had lived? In the new reality, her father, whom she hadn't seen in a decade, now lived as if he'd never separated from her mother. And the family's religious beliefs and lifestyles were all different. For Storey, it had been incredibly unnerving. For Eric, it was just plain fascinating. Who knew how many realities co-existed out there.

But time was wasting. He stepped through and grabbed up anything he thought Storey might need. Some larger sheets of paper folded within a smaller sketch book and a sweater. She'd had everything she needed for the last trip to the Louers' dimension, and as far as he remembered, she'd still had her travelling pouch during that last jump with his father. But…that didn't mean she still had it. He still had his packets. He checked to make sure, but they were both there. Good. Now what else could they need?

As he rummaged through her desk he found several of her granola bars. Perfect! He snatched them up and wondered at the sensibility of going downstairs for more food. She had to be hungry and not knowing how long they'd be before getting out, he crept down the stairs and into the kitchen. The room was empty. He pulled cupboards open and studied their contents. Nothing looked familiar. He shrugged, and started filling his package with anything that looked edible. Then he opened the fridge and grinned when he saw a block of cheese. Tammy would be in heaven. As would her pet, Skorky. Those two had eaten anything and everything, but especially cheese.

He snagged the block and several apples and decided he'd taken enough time. He slipped out the kitchen door and ran to the treed area. Once under cover, he coded in Paxton's lab. Within minutes he stood inside the normalcy of his world, his mentor still huddled over his key board.

"Any news?" He asked striding forward.

Paxton swiveled, his features brightening as he saw Eric. "No. Nothing."

Damn. Even as he registered the swear word, he realized using it no longer mattered. The simple rules he'd lived by all his life were overshadowed by the urgency of Storey's situation. "Then we have no option." He walked over to the monitor, noted the coordinates where Storey currently stood and punched them into his codex. "I'll send you a message as soon as I land."

Not giving Paxton a chance to argue, Eric walked to the portal station and hit the button on his codex to take him to Storey. The last thing he saw as the smoke rose quickly to take him away, was the stricken look on Paxton's face.

CHAPTER 6

S TOREY STARED AS Dillon stood on the paper. On, not *in*. She groaned. She *needed* the portals to work. "Stylus, it didn't work."

No. It can't.

"But I need it to work. This one was going to Paxton's lab. Would it be better to try for my dimension?" She searched through her packet for a portal to her bedroom.

No.

She sighed, trying hard to hold back the frustration and fear from overwhelming her. This couldn't be. "Okay," she said slowly thinking, "We came from the Louers' new dimension. Then it makes sense to return that way. That pathway has to be relatively fresh – as compared to one which Dillon traveled so long ago. So in theory, we should have an easier time going back there."

And she'd take that place over this one any day.

Silence.

"Correct?" She snapped, her voice sharper than she'd intended. Shit. Fear ate away at her nerves. She ran her fingers through her hair.

Possibly. We have no data to confirm that. Based on dimensional travel history, we do know it is easier to move through a pathway already forged.

Storey brightened. "Of course it is. Same as any path.

The person who walks in the lead breaks the path and the person who comes behind will be able to walk easier. So therefore, we should take the same way back to where I was. In the portal between the Louers' caves and Paxton's lab."

Excitement surged between her. She knew there'd be a way out of this. She just had to get her mind wrapped around the concept.

In theory.

She laughed. "Stylus, you are getting downright maudlin."

We do not like the lack of data. Decisions should be made on facts.

"Sure, but like you said," she added cheerfully, "We don't have any to go on. We will be the first. Therefore we are creating the data for you to store for others."

She couldn't be sure, but it was almost as if the air lightened. She grinned. There was more personality from the stylus every day. There *were* souls in there. Such a fascinating concept.

"Now to test that theory, we have to try from the point where we arrived in this dimension." She hesitated, then asked, "Do you agree with that logic?"

Yes.

She smiled, feeling much better. It always felt better to have others agree – even if they were both wrong. "Okay. So…we need to return to the physical location where we arrived. You have those coordinates."

Yes.

Storey turned to look at Dillon. He had fallen asleep again. On the damn paper. She sighed and nudged his shoulder. He slept on. She nudged him harder. "Dillon? Wake up."

He snuffled.

At least that's the way it sounded. Bizarre. "Dillon. It's time to go. Wake up please. I need to pick up that piece of paper."

Dillon opened his eyes. Looked down, and stepped back. "Sorry," he whispered. "So tired."

Returning wasn't looking so easy. Storey started to realize just how much of a problem she had on her hand. She didn't know if Dillon would survive the trip. The biggest concern was that his physical body couldn't handle the travel or even worse, couldn't handle another reality. Gravity, atmosphere, and whatever else was different here would suddenly impact a body held in stasis for over a century. His muscles – would they even hold him upright after all this time? If she managed to get him out of here would he collapse and die in her arms?

Was he better off here? He was alive this way. If his existence here was life. Maybe down the road, Paxton's people could create the technology to come back here and find Dillon.

No. He's almost gone.

Shit.

"I'm his only hope, aren't I?"

We believe so.

Believe? Such an odd word for the stylus. Everything the stylus had spoken of before had been definite, based on facts. It had been sure, almost computerized in its analysis of problems and optimal solutions. Until this mess. This was a new scenario for the stylus. And it had no answers. Only suggestions.

She shrugged. "First, we have to return to where we arrived in the In-between." And maybe in the meantime she'd come up with an answer. She spun around to reorient herself and grimaced. "Going back to where we arrived isn't going to be easy, is it?"

Consider this reality and your thoughts.

She paused and considered the stylus's words. And grinned. She scooped up the paper that Dillon had been standing on, grabbed Dillon's hand and closed her eyes. She took a deep breath and let it out slowly. Calmly. She thought herself back to the point where she'd arrived in the In-between. She let the knowledge that she could create her reality through her thoughts settle deeper into her psyche. Letting the memory resurface of having fallen because she'd imagined herself to be falling, and having stopped her fall because she'd told herself she'd stopped. Therefore she was back where she'd first arrived because she imagined herself to be.

With her eyes still closed, she asked, "Stylus, where are we?"

The stylus made a series of clicking noises then a long hum sounded. She didn't know if that was good or bad, but it felt…good.

We are back where we began.

She took several little steps for joy. "Perfect."

She glanced at the almost comatose Dillon at her side. "Are there others here in this dimension that I should be trying to save?"

We don't believe so.

"Can you run a scan and see? Maybe look for heat signatures. Something?"

We will do so. We can do more than search for heat signatures. And have been since we first landed.

"Good."

You are not alone.

She froze. "I have Dillon here, so I am not alone. Do you mean there is someone else here?"

A Toran.

She grinned. Then her grin fell off. "Of course there is a Toran. Dillon is here."

Dillon is a Louer.

"He's what?" she exclaimed. "He doesn't look anything like a Louer."

He is as they were originally.

Oh God. She stared in shock at Dillon. "But," she whispered, "He looks like Eric."

Eric is a Toran.

"So what's the difference?" She threw up her hands in frustration.

The faction they originated from.

Faction? Didn't that mean something political or religious in her world?

On Toran a faction is a Clan, a group formed of both family and political ties.

"So there were two groups of the same people. Half called themselves Torans and the other half called themselves Louers? The two fought, the Torans won and enslaved the Louers. The Louers fought back and were banished."

Yes.

Simple and sad. As she stared at Dillon, she realized he had to have been born after the war that enslaved the Louers. How had he been spared? "Stylus, how is it that Dillon is a Louer and free? Or was he a slave?"

He was free. No one knew he was a Louer. Dillon's name is in the database as having gone lost.

And his ancestors?

Again, a secret. Their ancestors were Louers that makes them Louers. Ancestral law states that you are of the same clan as your parentage. No one was allowed to change allegiance.

"But that's not fair," she cried. "Children have a right to choose what they believe. They shouldn't be punished by who their parents are."

Even as she said that, she could think of many instances in her own world where just that had happened and continued to happen. Those born into slavery, born in jail, born to different races. Each of those offspring had an uphill climb to get free of their heritage. It appeared to be no different here.

Unfortunately.

Shaking her mind free of those depressing thoughts and tucking the knowledge that Dillon was a Louer back into the corner of her mind, she turned to the more immediate issue.

"You said there is a Toran here. Who and where?"

Eric.

"Really?" she shouted. This time she danced around Dillon, joy rippling through every part of her. "We're saved!"

Dillon stared at her and blinked.

She groaned in disgust. "Dillon, it means someone is here to help us." She continued to skip in small circles. "I presume he's on his way to us? And we should stay until he finds us?"

He landed at our old coordinates, where you found Dillon.

She laughed. "I knew he'd find us. Does he have the new coordinates?"

Paxton has just given them to him.

"Good." She said with satisfaction. "Then he should be here any moment." Then she frowned. And tugged Dillon several steps over. "Just so he doesn't land on top of us."

She stared and stared at the spot. Nothing happened.

She glanced around in case he'd adjusted the coordinates slightly and still nothing. She turned back to look at the original spot.

And there was Eric.

His grin flashed, huge and full of relief.

"Woot!" She launched herself into his arms. "I knew you'd come!"

He picked her up and swung her around and around. "Oh, I'm so glad to see you."

He put her back down and gave her a blistering kiss.

She pulled back slightly and beamed up at him. "Maybe I'll have to disappear again, if you're going to welcome me like that!"

"Trust you." He glanced around. "Man is this is a weird place."

She snorted. "Tell me about it!"

He smiled down at her, then froze and spun around. "What the…"

"Yeah, what a surprise, huh?" Storey glanced at the sleeping Dillon. "I still don't understand that whole 45 degree angle sleeping thing."

"He's asleep?" Eric dropped his to a faint whisper. He bent over slightly to look closer.

"Yes. I think he's been asleep since he arrived. According to the stylus that was a long time ago." She shrugged. "He's spoken to me a couple of times, but then always nods off again."

"Unbelievable." Eric shook his head. "How did he survive here?"

Storey wished she knew. "I have no idea. I think he went into a sort of hibernation. The stylus doesn't think he'll survive if we try to take him home though. That his muscles, after not experiencing gravity in so long, won't support him. And that's just the beginning of the problems. The thing is, I can't leave him."

Eric stared down at her. "This isn't a Louer child to return to her parents. This is an adult male Toran. If he dies while going home, surely that's better than this quasi-dead existence."

That whole death with dignity thing. She sighed. "I hate to kill the poor man. And speaking of family," Storey winced, not sure how Eric would react. "He says he has a brother, named Paxton."

Eric's head swiveled to stare down at her in shock. Then back at Dillon. "It couldn't be."

"What?" When he didn't answer right away, Storey poked him in the chest. "What couldn't be?"

"Paxton did lose a brother when they were young men. He was playing up to the ladies while porting and fell In-between."

She gasped and turned to stare at Dillon. "Oh no. Then we definitely can't leave him."

"Neither do I want to take him home to his brother to die."

She didn't know what to say. "Stylus. Is there anything we can do for Dillon?"

His body won't be able to handle living in the other dimensions.

"But he's not alive here either," she said in frustration. Then caught Eric's look. Right. He couldn't hear the stylus.

Quickly she explained what she she'd heard. "According to the stylus, Dillon can't live in other dimensions, but it told me earlier he won't be able to survive much longer here, either. I don't want to believe that."

"But there is no other way." Eric wafted his arm in the thick soup. "Either desert him to this endless darkness or take him home and he will either live or die, but at least he'll be home again. Think of his family. This would mean tremendous closure for them."

Storey opened her mouth to speak, but a weird noise sounded.

What the hell was that?

A HEAVY DRONING noise, one Eric had initially taken to be a part of this strange space, increased like an amplifier steadily turning higher and higher.

"Storey, what is that?" He had to yell over the noise.

Then the noise cut off.

The look on Storey's face was…stunned. Yet…preoccupied?

"Storey? What's wrong?" No answer. Eric leaned in. Her gaze was intent, but focused inward. She had to be talking to the stylus. He'd seen that same look before. A part of him was jealous. To have that kind of connection – special.

Although, from looking at the contortions in Storey's face right now, he wasn't sure the process was particularly comfortable. He reached out and stroked her shoulder and upper arms. "Storey, are you okay?" He didn't expect an answer. In fact the air was so thick and dense, he had to wonder if there wasn't something else going on. He kept glancing at Dillon to see if he'd been affected by either the noise or the weird atmosphere, but Dillon just swayed in place.

Paxton's brother. After all this time. How could they help him? It would mean so much to Paxton.

With another helpless glance at Storey, Eric lifted his arm and sent a message to Paxton, letting him know what he'd found. The old tech communication system was one of the boosts Paxton had added to his codex – Toranese code. Awkward, but functional.

The answer was immediate.

Eric gave a short laugh as he read it off. *"Not possible."* He stared at Dillon for a long moment, realizing what a miracle it was that he should even be alive after all this time. It was as if time had stopped. So not possible. Yet the proof stood before him.

He painstakingly sent another message explaining that Dillon hadn't aged much in appearance, but appeared to exist in a semi-asleep state. Although capable of talking, he was confused. Writing on the codex was a slow and tedious process, but Eric did his best.

He added at the end that he didn't think Dillon could survive a return to any normal dimension.

Paxton replied, saying he'd confer with his stylus. Maybe they could come up with answers.

And that's when Eric remembered the big broken stylus he'd brought with him. He reached for it. As his fingers touched it, he realized the stylus was vibrating. He pulled it out to rest on his hand. The vibration pulsed so strongly the stylus physically rocked.

Damaged maybe. Dead…nope. It was foreign in a way. He hadn't had much to do with the styluses and this was the only one he'd touched that didn't burn him. Although there was a warning heat, it wasn't enough to force him to put it away. "Still trying to send out a warning aren't you? But you're not strong enough. What was I thinking in bringing you? How much help can you be in this state?"

"B…igg…er, tha…n you—"

Eric stared as Storey tried to speak again, but the words wouldn't come. "Storey?"

But she'd gone quiet again.

Too quiet. He stared into her eyes. All he saw was a reflection of the same look…from Dillon's eyes.

CHAPTER 7

STOREY REELED UNDER an onslaught of emotion and sound. It pounded at her from all sides. At first she'd been too slammed to understand. Then a pattern had formed in her mind. It wasn't just one external voice, it was two, with several conversations going on at once. She'd heard her stylus before. Many times. Its communication had an essence to it, a flavor that was her stylus. And that made it very distinctive from the other thoughts floating in her head. Plus it spoke with a certain rhythm. A different structure to the sounds. But now there was a new voice.

Speaking to the stylus and sometimes…maybe to her.

It wasn't Eric, though wouldn't it be cool if they could speak like that. She shuddered as another wave washed through her mind. She caught bits and pieces. Not that she understood them, but there was something recognizable and yet foreign at the same time in the interaction between the voices in her mind. She didn't dare get hung up on the concept of voices in her head. In her dimension she'd be seeing a shrink for that. In Eric's dimension…she had no idea. Most people couldn't get their mind wrapped around such things.

For herself, well…apparently she was different. And the longer she stayed out of her normal life, the more odd she became. Or at least the more aware she was of her differences.

A particularly sharp tone in her mind made her close her eyes. She knew Eric was trying to talk to her. But about what defeated her.

He pulled something out of his pocket. She wanted to laugh hysterically when the object registered in her sore brain. A broken stylus. *The* broken stylus.

Yes. Me.

Whoa. What was that…who was that?

"Are you speaking to me?" she asked out loud. She managed to shake her head slightly at Eric, hoping he'd understand that she wasn't talking to him. Carrying on internal and external conversations at the same time was impossible at the best of times; right now, though…

Yes.

"Are you my stylus?" Even though she knew it couldn't be, she had to ask.

No.

Then her stylus spoke. *He is our leader. You rescued him. We are grateful.*

Oh my God. She was speaking to the broken stylus.

That is correct.

Now she didn't know who had said that.

We did.

She'd have laughed if she could have. At the moment, she couldn't tell the two styluses apart. And that wasn't right. She had a connection to her stylus. This broken stylus defied the Torans' belief about bonding and communication. Or had it?

No.

She sighed. *So how then?*

The bonding increases the abilities between the holder and the soul bound stylus. Our broken leader is the best of us. He can speak slightly without being bonded.

Storey had to think about that. *What about the Louers? They have telecommunication. Why couldn't they speak to you? The Broken One was there.*

To communicate both parties must be open. The Louers lost many in the early years after they were banished. Much knowledge has been lost. The survivors over time discarded the styluses as childhood toys, broken and forgotten. Not as instruments of value. They would not see a stylus as something desirable. Or the souls within as valuable. If they even knew that we were within.

She shared the information with Eric.

"How sad." Eric frowned at her.

She nodded. This communication system was cumbersome. "Stylus, can you speak with Eric?"

Eric shook his head.

No. He is not open to such a form of communication.

Right. She asked, "Can't you two speak out loud so he can hear?"

No. We are not allowed to speak in such ways.

"Not allowed?" She pounced on that term. "But it is possible?"

A buzz hummed through her ear. And she realized they were speaking together, but not with her. So although she understood they were talking, she couldn't hear the conversation.

"Broken one, what do I call you?"

Broken one.

She winced. *Have you no name?*

I was once called Barrat. Many years ago.

A slow smile spread across her face. "Barrat. Lovely

name. Are there more of you in there?"

No.

"That is unusual, is it not?"

Yes.

"And lonely," she suggested, sad for him.

Yes.

"Do you know how to help us leave In-between?" she asked.

That buzz filled the air as the two stylus started again. While they were at it, she caught Eric up on what she'd learned.

"If they figure out something – good. Otherwise, since the longer we stay here the harder it may be to get out, I suggest we try leaving now." Eric pulled a second codex out from his pack and clicked it on Storey's wrist. Then digging into his pants pocket he pulled out a third. "I thought I was over doing it bringing more than two units, but now…" He stepped up to Dillon, snapped the instrument around Dillon's wrist in one smooth move. He needn't have worried. Dillon continued to sleep, swaying gently on his feet.

"How bizarre," he said, unconsciously mimicking her earlier words.

"I know." But to business. "Where are we travelling to?"

"Paxton's lab?" He cocked his head at her. "I know my father did this to you, but I hope you won't hold all of us to blame."

She just gave him a long look. "Never. And as long as I don't have to see your father again…all is good." Glancing around she shivered and added, "Besides, any place is better than here." Then she remembered something else. "The stylus said it would be easier for me to leave by heading back the way I'd arrived. I planned on drawing a portal back to the Louers' new dimension. Although we were closer to arriving at Paxton's lab when I was pushed out than the Louers' dimension."

He blinked.

She glared. "Don't do that. That's what Dillon always does."

"Sorry. I'm just trying to figure out what you're talking about."

"Oh, never mind." She threw up her hands. "Let's just get on with it. But first, Stylus, did you two figure out how to get us out?"

The Broken One says he knows, but is trying to access his archives. He is damaged.

That again. "Okay Eric, let's try your way."

He shrugged. "Good. The sooner the better. This place is…weird." He tugged her closer to Dillon and made sure they were all crowded up tight together, then at his timing, they hit the buttons on the multiple codexes. Dillon just swayed in place, seemingly unaware of what was going on around him.

To Storey's relief, the black smoke swelled up around them. "Yeah, we're going home!"

"And how many times have we thought that in the past," Eric said with a grin, his head so close she could feel his breath against her hair.

"I know. I just want to go home and stay there."

"Speaking of which, I went to your house and grabbed more sketchbooks before coming to get you."

"Oh," she gasped. "How was it? Did you see my parents?"

"No. And, I think it was normal. Your room looked like

it did in the beginning. There were no vehicles there and I didn't see anyone in the house."

"But my room looked the same?" How odd. She wanted things back to the way they were supposed to be, but she hadn't been that lucky yet. "Stylus, you did say fixing my home dimension was an easy job, right?"

Not easy, but possible. And the dimension will need to be realigned.

"Uh Oh. What does that mean?"

You will have to port out while the changes happen and port back in afterwards.

"How do I do that?"

Go to the closest dimension and then come back in.

Her stomach sank. "The Louers' dimension?" She felt Eric stiffen beside her. Neither of them wanted to go back there again. Quickly she related the conversation so far.

Yes.

"Can we port to Eric's dimension instead?"

No. Not without more of us. We are damaged.

"Damn. I'm getting really sick of hearing that."

She'd been using the conversation to distract her from the portal travel and the fact that the mist hadn't dissipated. "Eric?"

"It's fine. Don't forget there are three of us here."

"And three codexes," she reminded him. "So lots of power."

"But not for this pea soup stuff. I expected it to take longer as the air is so different."

She was prepared to be patient. She was just so happy to have him with her. She'd been afraid she'd be lost alone forever. And that reminded her of someone else that had become very dear to her. "I wonder how Tammy is doing?"

"I'm sure she's fine."

She tilted her head back. "Do you really think so?"

He smiled down, the curve of his lips barely visible. "Knowing Tammy, she's having lots of fun."

Storey wanted to believe it. The last thing she'd seen in Tammy's face had been happiness with the man who held her in his arms and sadness at saying good bye to Storey. Or Torrey as she'd called her. "I'm sure Tammy was trying to talk to us telepathically in the portal that last time."

"She probably was. We know they have a higher developed internal communication system than we do."

On a whim, Storey closed her eyes sent out a loud greeting, "Hi Tammy."

Nothing. Then she hadn't expected there to be a response. They were somewhere In-between. Eric thought he knew what he was doing, but she was afraid this whole return to Paxton's lab wasn't happening. She opened her eyes. Black mist continued to surround them. She sighed. "Eric, I don't think we're going anywhere."

He lifted his arm to look at his brightly lit codex. "We're not at the same place we were however."

She brightened. "Oh good. As long as we're going somewhere. So do we just wait?"

"For a bit longer." He slung an arm through Dillon's. "I don't want to lose him again."

"Again?"

"Let me rephrase that. I want to make sure we get him home to Paxton safe and sound. For however long he's got."

"Right. Stylus, where are we?"

In-between.

"Still?"

Yes.

Damn. "But we are at a different point in In-between than we were before – correct?"

Correct.

Good. She smiled happily.

Ten minutes later she wasn't so happy. Nothing had changed. "Why do I get the feeling that we are caught in this portal now?"

"I'm thinking you might be right." Eric tapped his codex several times.

Storey watched him. "Can you change our destination while we're in here?"

"No."

She didn't want to bug, but this was getting them nowhere. Literally. "Isn't there a reset button or something?"

"I reset it a few moments ago," he admitted. "I don't think it changed anything."

"Great." So not. "Okay Stylus, are we still traveling?"

Yes.

Good. She lifted a hand to massage her temple. So much to consider. "Which is the closest dimension for us to land first?"

Louers' dimension.

"Fine. I'm happy to land in the Louers' dimension if it gets us out of the pea soup." She cocked her head in question up at Eric. He shrugged. Right. It's not like they had much in the way of choice.

"Stylus, can you help us land there then?"

Yes.

She grinned. "Good. Do I need to do anythi—"

Musical sounds filled the air. Eric lifted his arm as the codex flashed and sounded off in a weird sequence. "I've never seen anything like this before."

"Hope I never do again." But if it improved their situation, she was good. "Stylus? What are you doing?"

The Broken One is doing this.

She gulped. "Broken one? What are you doing?"

Changing the communication system to accept new coordinates. I have no other souls to help. I can only use what I have.

"Okay," she said slowly, "And that means what?"

There is a destination point In-between that we used to establish portal travel in the beginning. But my archives have only some of it listed. We need it all to be able to chart our way out.

"Oh, that's the whole point of origin thing," she said in excitement. "What do you need to heal yourself?"

Eric rolled his eyes at her. It had to be hard with the half conversation stuff.

"More souls."

She groaned. "And how do I help you get those?

Silence.

"And even if I had another soul for you, how would they go into the stylus? Your stylus form is broken."

I would need to transfer to a new stylus.

Talk about mind boggling.

To transfer from one stylus to the next, we must have a third that is open to both sets of souls inside. A middleman. Both stylus souls join in the consciousness of the middleman. Then the old soul joins with the soul of the new stylus and transfers with it back to the stylus.

The Broken One's voice sounded thin and reedy as she listened. But his explanation sounded reasonable. And weird. But doable in a freaky way. "But how did the first soul get into each stylus originally?

We were sent In-between.

In-between? She shouted. "What? You sent souls to In-between then brought them back inside the new stylus?"

"Yes."

<hr>

ERIC STARED IN shock at Storey's excited telling of what she'd just learned. That it was not reasonable nor feasible didn't seem to deter her.

"That's why all this technology has been lost. The Broken One was broken before his information could be downloaded to the archives. That's why you have so few styluses and no new ones. No one knew how to make new ones nor how to add new souls to old styluses." She danced in place, her hair bobbed with each hop she was so excited.

Could it be? Surely not. Eric looked around the fog that still surrounded them and had to wonder. They'd had little information on the styluses until Storey had dropped into their lives. Literally. And if she was right, what did it mean about them and their situation? Had people come and returned from In-between as people, or only as styluses? 'Cause he really didn't want to spend eternity inside a pencil.

At least not until he'd thoroughly enjoyed his current life. Dare he ask? He almost didn't want to know the answer, but given the situation… "Storey, can the Broken One tell you if anyone has successfully left In-between…not in a stylus?"

The smile fell from her lips as she understood what he was saying. An instant shadow of horror whispered across her expressive face.

"Don't assume we can't get out any other way." He rushed to say. "Let's find out for sure first."

She nodded slowly. Her gaze landed on Dillon as her mind, the fastest he'd ever seen, seem to flit from one answer to another. "It could be the saving grace for Dillon."

He turned to look at the sleeping man beside them. If that was possible, it would be one answer. He didn't know that Paxton would consider it a good one though.

Still, they didn't have much choice.

"Ask them. Ask them if Dillon could be moved to a stylus and if we can escape – with our bodies."

CHAPTER 8

STOREY'S INITIAL EXCITEMENT drained as if a switch had been flicked. Her emotions were all over the board. Living in a stylus might be an option for Dillon. But she didn't know how much of a good idea that was, transferring his soul to an inanimate object, given he was a young man who'd not had a chance to live yet.

But if death was the only other option… She quickly called out to both styluses mentally. *Can Dillon join a stylus? He's been here a long time, but according to my stylus he can no longer live in any of the other three dimensions.*

It's possible, said the Broken One. *Once safe, his soul will recuperate. Be as he was.*

In theory that was good news. But… *Are you both happy with your decision to be in a stylus? Is this something to be enjoyed or feared? I guess I'm asking if we would be doing him a favor or punishing him?*

It is an honor among us to assist in the continuation of our species.

And that's where she had trouble. They'd actually been continuing the existence of their enemies. Weren't they? Or did it not matter as they were in essence one species? Then she'd have to include the people from her own dimension as well. They were all essentially the same. She didn't doubt there were some differences, maybe even at the DNA level, but as far as she could see, Dillon, Eric and herself were all the same people.

Exactly.

She nodded thoughtfully. "And yet only Louers are soul bound to the styluses?"

Yes.

Interesting. She wondered on the perspective of each soul going into this arrangement. Still, for Dillon it might be the best answer. If not the only one.

"What do we need to do for Dillon to join a stylus? Can he join one of yours or do we need a completely different one? He is a new soul and you both need those, right?"

Yes.

From the look of understanding on Eric's face he was following the one sided conversation. "Eric, did you bring more styluses?"

He shook his head.

He need not have one with him. The process is in the porting home. He would be outfitted with a destination that is inside the target stylus.

"Cool." She laughed at Eric's frown and explained. The look of astonishment that followed made her grin. "Yeah, simple, isn't it.

Eric gave a half snort, half laugh. "The concept is simple. But we're missing just a little bit of information. Like how do we get the coordinates of the destination stylus? If we give the coordinates for where a stylus is at any given point, the person will land beside not inside it."

"They appear to want a coordinate from the inside of the stylus. With that information, would it work?"

He stared at her. "I have no idea. I have never heard sending people inside of something."

"Of course, you haven't," Storey said gently. "You didn't even know there were souls inside these instruments. This information has been lost to your people for a long time. Even Paxton isn't likely to know."

The Broken One said, *He does now. I spoke to his stylus.*

She titled her head. "Broken One, if you can speak to Paxton's stylus, why is it you couldn't speak to them from the Louers' dimension? And don't tell me you are damaged."

I was in hibernation. When you rescued me, your Stylus, as you call him, contacted me to see if I was safe. That started the waking process.

"And now you are functioning, but damaged. Right?"

Silence.

Then a hesitant voice that she had yet to hear from her stylus said, *We said you would help him.*

"Help him?" Storey frowned. What could she possibly do?

You can speak with us. Directly. With me, the Broken One said.

"I'm not sure how, but yes, that is apparently what we are doing."

I am using the connection between your stylus and myself, and by extension your stylus and you, to communicate with you.

"You can do that? Wow."

It is you who has made this possible. I thank you.

There was a lot of thanking going on and somehow Storey suspected there was something they wanted from her.

You are correct.

Storey…the Broken One needs to be saved. He is important to us.

"So you've said." A niggling suspicion had her stomach twisting tighter and tighter. Somehow she didn't think she was going to like what was coming. She held her breath.

We need you to save him.

She almost laughed. She'd saved him once already. What more could she do?

"Storey? What's going on? You look…ill." Eric's voice intruded into her confusion.

She took a deep breath and tried to reassure him. "Not really. My stylus wants me to save the Broken One."

In sync the two stared down at the stylus in Eric's hand. "How? It's damaged."

There was that word again. She wanted to hit him. She groaned instead. "Don't you use that word, too. I know it's broken. Damaged. In need of souls or whatever. But in this case, they want something specific. I just not sure what. Or how."

"Can't we just send a soul to this stylus?" He looked thunderstruck as he realized what he'd just said. "I didn't just say that, did I?"

"Absolutely, you did." She laughed. "See, it's almost normal to think this way."

"We don't have souls to give the Broken One, do we?" He winced. "I can't imagine forcing someone to this life. It would be essentially murder."

She shook her head. "That's why they used slaves. And some were happy to do this. I imagine others…not so much. And no, we don't have any other souls. Just Dillon. But I don't think that's the answer. From what I'm understanding the stylus itself is damaged. And not only can we not add a new soul, the Broken One needs to be moved to a different stylus or be lost altogether."

Eric reared back. "Is that even possible?"

As she thought back on the muddled conversations, she

thought she just might understand. "I think…they want me to allow the Broken One to join with me, then through the bond I already have with my stylus, travel to my stylus. Using me as a middleman of some kind. A conduit, maybe."

"What? No way."

"It might be possible." She shrugged. "I'm just not sure what's involved and how dangerous it might be."

"Dangerous? That's it. You're not doing it." He shook his head violently, his hair flying out every which way. She loved the way he hooked his hands on his hips and widened his stance. So manly. And so not going to stop her.

"I don't know that it is or isn't yet. I'm only guessing here."

It is. That was her stylus speaking. *And you are correct. That is what we ask of you.*

She winced inside, careful to keep her reaction hidden from Eric. What he didn't know and all that. *How dangerous?* She kept the communication internal this time.

Silence.

Of course they didn't know. *How long will it take?*

Minutes, said her stylus.

That is for the first part of the process, added the Broken One. *The second stage will take slightly longer. This is new. We have information that it is possible. But I haven't done this process. I must learn too.*

Oh boy. *Does that mean you will be inside me? Cause that's very freaky.*

Yes. That is the only way.

She barely held back a shudder. She didn't know why it bothered her. Normally, she'd bend over to help someone in need, but this seemed more…private…more personal Almost invasive, and yet she was speaking to them mentally anyway. How much different would it be?

Not much different. Your discomfort would be small… The Broken One hesitated, before admitting softly, *And my need is great.*

We would honor your sacrifice.

That word gave her the willies. Made her afraid there was more to this process that she wasn't seeing.

Eric interrupted her private concerns. "Paxton is worried about losing his brother again."

"Which way? In a stylus or by him returning to the dimension?"

"Both. Dillon will die if we take him home. But as the concept of souls bound inside a stylus is foreign to him, he's afraid his brother would be upset at waking up inside a stylus."

"Why don't we ask him?" She shrugged, "What can it hurt?"

She turned to Dillon and shook his shoulder. Dillon swayed in place, his hands hanging slightly forward. "Dillon, we need to talk."

Dillon looked at her, that same blank stillness on his features. Then his gaze cleared suddenly. "What?"

"We spoke with your brother, Paxton," she tried not to let her impatience show, but she really wanted to leave this place. And in order to do that they needed some answers. "We would like to take you back to him, but there is a problem." She tried to peer into his eyes. Make sure he was understanding, following her words so far. His big doe eyes gave her no clue, but there was something going on in there.

"I can't go back," he whispered. "It's been too long."

She winced. "I'm afraid that might be true. We can't know for sure."

"I thought it many times." His big eyes pleaded with her. "For so long. I don't want to be held a prisoner here…lost forever."

Oh boy. "That's why I wondered about another solution. You can't go back and you don't want to stay here, do you remember styluses from when you lived with Paxton? These instruments." She pulled hers loose from her shirt so he could see it.

His gaze locked on it, brightened. A look of recognition came over him. "You are one of the blessed. My brother too, the head of his field, was gifted with one such as this."

"Yes, I am blessed because of my stylus. But that's not what I meant. Inside these styluses are souls. Like you and me." At Eric's stifled snort, she shot him dark look. "They were willing to spend eternity alive, inside such an instrument to help their people, your people, develop into the future. Whatever that may be."

Dillon shook his head, she could almost hear the bones protesting the movement. "No. Not possible. It is an instrument. Only."

"Yes it is, but it is made powerful by the souls inside.

"Uh, Storey?" Eric called, "I don't think this is working."

She frowned. "Damn it. I just thought that maybe he would like to make a choice here. Death, stay here for the rest of eternity, or bond to a stylus and spend eternity being of use. He lost his entire life here. Wouldn't he prefer to salvage something from this?"

"But if he doesn't understand, he can't make that decision. And I'm afraid that understanding is beyond him at this point."

"For so long, I was angry, then sad that I should be forgotten and lost." Dillon said, his voice faltering and thin, but the adamant thread was clear. "I would like to have my life back."

"And that we can't give you." Storey said earnestly, "but we can give you a meaningful existence. Just not one you might expect."

Dillon blinked, his gaze slowly going from her to Eric to the stylus and back to her again. "You are serious."

"She is very serious." Eric stepped forward. "You would find a life of value, of contribution and bonding with other people and souls. Except you would only exist in soul form and be contained in a stylus."

"In other words you would physically be dead. Your soul would live on and interact on a daily basis with the people around you and technically, with your brother."

Dillon straightened. "Paxton. I could communicate with him?"

Storey looked at Eric. "There's no reason why he couldn't, is there? Paxton speaks with his stylus now on a regular basis and his stylus communicates with other styluses?"

Eric nodded. "True, but maybe confirm that with your stylus."

Right. "Am I right, stylus? Can Dillon speak with his brother once in the stylus?"

Yes. It will take a little time for him to adapt. But he will be able to communicate with us all.

"Dillon the stylus says you will be able to communicate with the whole community of them. You will be one of them."

Dillon smiled, a slow birthing of hope, and said. "I would like that."

ERIC'S HEAD SPUN as communication surged around him and over him. Stuck In-between, so thick in fog, he dared not step back. But he wanted to. To take a moment and regroup. But Storey was speaking with both styluses and they were speaking with Paxton's stylus who was in turn keeping Paxton and then Eric on top of what was happening.

Paxton had the suggested recipient stylus in his hands. He had coded in the destination coordinates to the database, given by the Broken One and with the Broken One's help had downloaded the coordinates of the other styluses to the archives. Now the transfer was ready from Paxton's end.

Eric wasn't sure where his end was at. He'd tried to watch Storey, but the multiple facial reactions as she alternately understood or didn't understand what was being said telepathically fascinated him. He wanted to ask questions, but knew he'd slow the process down. It was better to wait it out.

He was happy that something was happening at last. They'd been standing here long enough. He wanted to leave this foggy half world and never come back. But he also wanted to make sure he got everyone home safe. He just didn't know if that was possible yet.

Paxton, once he'd heard Dillon's comment, had been all for the transfer. The Broken One had chosen the stylus most in need, but had emphasized that all needed new souls sooner rather than later.

He snorted at that.

"What Eric?" Storey asked, fatigue showing on her face. "Is something wrong?"

He smiled down at her. She looked so valiant right now, tired and wanting to be anywhere else but here, yet still game to do what she could to help others out. Even if it was dangerous. And he had no doubt it was. He also knew he wouldn't be able to talk her out of it.

She had this belief that she could do anything. So far she had, but life tended to deliver a major reality crash at some point. Not a reality check, but a complete flat out brick-to-the-face realization that you couldn't save everyone or everything.

"Are you sure you want to do this?" He tried to keep the worry out of his voice, but her reassuring smile said he hadn't been as successful as he'd hoped.

"I feel like I need to."

"You don't," he exploded. "Let someone else do this."

"Who?" she reached out a palm and cupped his cheek. He leaned into her soft touch. She was the most compassionate, caring female he'd ever known. So giving. And so resourceful. He both admired and cared about her. Too much to let her get hurt.

He'd come here to make sure she got out safe. But what did getting out safe mean if she walked right into another dangerous situation?

"Don't be so worried." Storey gave his cheek a pat before withdrawing her hand. "I'll be fine."

He frowned at her. She reached up and kissed his cheek.

"Will you?" he asked, his voice deepening with his heightened emotions, "Because I'm not sure I can take it if you aren't."

Her beautiful eyes darkened. She stepped back and said, "I will, but I think we need to help Dillon now."

Eric nodded, his stomach sinking with dread. "Yes, it's time." He lifted his right arm. "I have the coordinates here on my spare." He stepped around Storey and unhooked the codex on Dillon's arm and attached the properly coded one. There was a soft snick and it locked in place.

He stepped back, looking for any awareness from Paxton's brother of what was happening. Dillon's eyes were closed and once again he appeared to be sleeping. "Dillon, I've just put a codex on your arm. We're going to send you to the interior of the stylus now."

Dillon's lids fluttered. He nodded. His mouth opened, the words so faint Eric had to bend closer to hear. The words trickled out. "Not feeling too good."

Eric could just imagine. This needed to happen fast. Dillon was fading quickly. He shot a warning glance at Storey. He nodded in Dillon's direction. "The codex is set. He's running out of time."

A frown mingled with the worry twisting Storey's features. "I hope he lasts long enough to make the transition."

"Yeah, tell me again – how does he leave his body and go into the stylus? I'm just a little confused on that point."

She grimaced. "Actually so am I. Honestly I'm not sure I want to know, either. If this works then we've saved a life and reunited Paxton with his long lost brother."

She stepped slightly backwards. "I think we probably need to give him some room."

Eric lifted a brow, but retreated several steps, staying close to Storey. It was too easy to get lost in the fog. So thick he couldn't see more than a half dozen feet in front of him.

"Okay, now what?"

She looked over at him. And shrugged. "I don't know."

CHAPTER 9

S TOREY, AFTER MAKING sure Eric was what she hoped was a safe distance away, closed her eyes and asked, "What's next?"

Now we need to have Paxton run the program that will separate Dillon from his physical body and send him to the inside of his new stylus.

"I don't understand how this is possible. But if it's the only option…"

It became possible centuries ago, when some of the Toran and Louers developed psychic abilities involving astral travel. Much research and many experiments later, this was a process that could be followed by others.

Her insides locked down at the visual presented in her mind. Storey didn't know what to believe and her experience with styluses had her pondering life…and death. If death was only the end of the physical body in Eric's dimension, as proven by the people soul bound to the stylus, was that the same in her world? Was there something after death?

She didn't have time to work the angles in her mind, but realized at some point she'd have to sit down and clarify what this meant to her. And to her mother. It also showed her how lacking in beliefs she was. Without a strong religious background giving her defining guidelines one way or the other, she hadn't formulated any theories about death and afterlife herself. And now she'd experienced something so foreign to her world, that she knew she'd have no one else to discuss this with down the road. And that was sad.

"Storey?"

She took a deep breath. This so wasn't the time. With an attempt at a reassuring smile, she nodded. "Yes, let's do this."

The codex on Dillon's wrist started a series of notes that she'd never heard before. The sound achingly sad and heartbreakingly beautiful. Almost funeral. She spun a look at Eric and realized he was just as surprised as she was.

She watched as Dillon slowly appeared to sink in on himself. Fascinating. His features dimmed, his body slowly becoming fuzzy around the edges.

She'd expected the black mist to circle him and it did, but it seemed softer, more cloud like than she'd seen before. Instead of a hard port, dragging the body away to a new dimension, it was baby's breath gentle.

Tears welled up inside as she realized this was the end of Dillon as she'd known him. She could only hope he was traveling to somewhere so much better.

The music slowly faded as if moving a long way away. And it probably was. The fuzzy mist darkened to the point she could barely see anything within its depths.

Eventually the music died altogether. She waited. Would the mist disappear too?

It did, slowly. Dillon appeared to sway in place, then almost in slow motion his body disintegrated with the mist. Leaving nothing behind. Unfreakin' believable. And un-freakin' beautiful.

She was moved beyond tears. A warm hand wrapped around her shoulders.

"Are you okay?"

She smiled tremulously. "Yes. Or at least I will be soon."

"How long do you think before we know if it was successful?"

She'd like to know that herself.

"Stylus? Do you know if Dillon has arrived?"

He has.

A smile broke free, and Storey released the breath she'd held unconsciously. "Dillon is there."

"Really?" Eric's happy gasp made her laugh.

"Yes." Even she could hear the relief wreathing her voice as she asked, "Stylus, is he all right? Is he awake? Talking?"

Not yet. He will need time to acclimatize.

That wiped the smile off. "Any idea how long?" She reached up and squeezed Eric's hand at the worry etched on his features. Again, he couldn't hear all of the conversation. She gave him a thumbs up gesture.

He settled back slightly and waited.

This is an unknown. Depends on how long he needs to recuperate.

"Okay. Let me know, please, when anything changes."

She turned to Eric and relayed the information.

He shrugged. "We've done what we could for him. Now it's out of our hands. Do you think we can leave?" He looked around and shuddered. "I'd like to get out of here."

"Me too." She took a deep breath. "Stylus, what about us? Can we leave now?"

A heavy buzz filled the air.

A quick glance confirmed Eric heard it to. "I presume that's the styluses talking again. Not sure why that hum is so loud."

"If it helps us escape, I don't mind."

We don't know if the transfer for the Broken One will work in the physical dimensions.

Uh oh. Her next problem had appeared. "Eric, the styluses are not sure that the Broken One will be able to transfer in the regular dimensions. I believe they think the process might be easier if we do it here. They've always done the stylus transfers from In-between."

Not easier. But possible.

"Actually, they don't think the transfer can happen at all unless we do it here."

"So that's next?" His arm fell away, and he took several steps back. "Are you sure?"

"Yes."

She took a deep breath. "Okay, Stylus. What do we need to do?"

You don't need to do anything. Except remain calm.

Calm. That so wasn't easy. "Okay. I'm calm. Go ahead."

We need you to empty your mind. Just relax.

Empty my mind? How is that possible? she replied mentally, not wanting to worry Eric.

It will be easier for you if you are not trying to follow the process consciously.

Easier how?

There won't be a headache.

As soon as he mentioned the word, pain struck her on the back of the neck. She collapsed to her knees and held her head in her hands. "Ohhh," she moaned. "My head. It feels like it's going to explode."

Eric dropped beside her. He held her close. "Is this from the transfer?"

She writhed in place as the headache built higher, pounded louder, heavier.

She buried her face against Eric's shoulder shuddering in

pain. "I don't know," she whispered. "I think so."

"Jesus." He leaned his cheek on the top of her head. "How long will this take?"

"No idea." Then she couldn't speak at all. A small cry escaped her lips. The pressure built and built until she couldn't stand to be touched. She fell back, away from Eric. "Don't…"

"Storey," he came closer, his hands out in front of him. "Please, tell me. What can I do to help?"

"Don't touch. My nerves. Sensitized." She gasped loudly. "So much pain."

"How long? Stylus? How much longer?" Eric shouted. "It's too much. She can't take this."

She groaned and swayed back and forth still on her knees. "Oh my God. It's getting worse."

She collapsed to the ground and curled into a tight fetal position.

ERIC HAD NEVER felt so helpless. He reached out to touch Storey, then let his hands drop away. If he couldn't help her and couldn't talk to the stylus through her, he still had Paxton. He lifted his codex and sent a message to Paxton, first checking to see about Dillon, then checking to see if he could get answers on Storey.

The wait for a response seemed interminable. When it came, he jumped to read the message. *No idea on Dillon. According to the coordinates, he has arrived. There is mass there. I can see it on the monitor.*

"Well, thank heavens for something."

His codex flashed again. *The transfer is in progress.*

"It's killing Storey," he responded to the empty air.

"She's in terrible pain." There was no point in telling Paxton that. Neither of them could do anything to help. But he might know how long this was going to take. At least it was worth asking. But Paxton's response was no help. He had no idea.

"Damn."

Right about now, it would help to communicate with a stylus himself. He asked Paxton to check with his stylus.

Paxton wrote back: *I can't communicate with my stylus at this moment. They need everyone right now for this transfer. I don't understand it, but there is a horrific hum to the air.*

So it was a group effort.

According to Storey's stylus, they were trying to save a revered leader. Eric had no idea how they could have a leader amongst them. The thought that they could gather together, have a hierarchy, a society of styluses, really blew his mind.

He knew Storey would tell him off for denying them a community. And there was no doubt that's what they'd built.

Who'd have thought?

Just then Storey gave a high pitched squeal. Her head was thrown back on her neck into a rigid, backward arch. Her mouth opened and she screamed again. A long, painful wailing.

And then she fell silent. And still.

CHAPTER 10

STOREY SLOWLY CAME awake. She lifted her lids ever so slightly and realized that much hadn't changed. She was still in In-between, caught in the never ending mist. She slammed her eyes shut again. So what was different? She considered it slowly. Inside was different. Her breath still went in and out in a relaxed rhythm. Her temperature appeared normal. She couldn't feel pain anymore, so that was good. Whatever had been tearing her skull in two was gone. She rolled her head to one side experimentally. That worked well. Hesitantly, she lifted her head to look around.

Eric was crouched in front of her, worry lines marring his face.

"How do you feel now?"

She opened her mouth. No words came out. She tried again. Nothing. She frowned. Why did she have no voice? She coughed and heard the hoarse sounds coming from a long ways off. So her vocal cords worked. She tried again. "Aggh." She waggled her tongue inside her mouth. It felt larger, thicker than normal. Filling her mouth unnaturally full. Odd.

"Storey? You're scaring me." Such concern, caring, poured from his gaze. As if by his emotion alone he could fix whatever was wrong.

She managed a weak smile. "I'm…here." That sounded

better. Maybe she just needed a little more recovery time. She tried to sit up, managing to get her arm under her to prop herself up. Her arm gave way and she collapsed.

"Here, let me help." Eric grasped her under the arms and helped her to a sitting position. "Is that better?"

She nodded.

"You're having trouble talking?" Eric stared down into her eyes. She brightened and nodded.

A brush of relief whispered across his face. "Okay. What about the rest? Can you take a moment and check out the rest of you? Can you move? Think on your own? Is the Broken One in there with you?

"Yes."

Storey's eyes opened so wide they hurt. She stared at Eric.

That hadn't been her voice.

That had been a man's voice.

Oh no.

She swallowed heavily.

"Storey? Was that you?" Eric leaned back and stared. "Or was that the Broken One speaking?"

"Yes."

Eric lifted a brow. "Yes, what?"

"The Broken One speaks."

Storey shuddered. God what a feeling. Her vocal cords rippled, her mouth moved, only she wasn't the one moving them. She wasn't the one in control. The Broken One had control.

Stylus!

Yes.

What is going on? she asked. *The Broken One is speaking using my body. You didn't say he would be able to control my body while he was in me.*

I did not know it would happen.

Well it did, she snapped. *Now I need to move him from me to you. I can't function like this.*

There is some rest time required. This first move took much energy.

Then recharge. Fast.

It takes time. We are damaged.

She wanted to scream at that last phrase. *I know you are damaged. That's why we are doing this. But I am struggling here. How do I regain control?*

You never lost it. He is a visitor only.

And she, like a good host, had stepped aside. So he hadn't taken control – she'd handed it over. She closed her eyes and took a deep breath, letting it out slowly, softly in a long, meditative, drawn out sigh, releasing the old, dead air from her lungs.

As the last of the air exhaled, she smiled, feeling tension she hadn't been aware of drifting from her body. She felt…wonderful.

And peaceful.

Complete.

And that last thought scared the crap out of her.

Stylus…what is happening? I'm getting a little nervous here.

You have joined…us. Bonded to us all. Your soul knows it. Craves it, and now has that sense of belonging. You are one of us.

As the wonder and the shock of this revelation penetrated her confusion, she became aware of yet something else strange. A pain, running down the side of her neck and across her collarbone and back down her shoulder blade. She wanted to rub it, but at the same time it had a heat to it that made her pause. Even as her attention centered on the pain, it drifted away. As if her awareness of its existence was enough to remove it.

So not possible, but she wished it were.

It is.

She froze. That was the Broken One speaking – she thought. Hard to tell, as his mental voice was different than when he'd spoken from his previous location from inside the stylus.

It is I.

She nodded her head slowly, gaining confidence that the pain really was gone. *Are you saying I will be able to heal myself now? That's not possible – is it?*

None of this should be possible, but apparently she'd been wrong about that, too. She had the Broken One inside her physical body and if that didn't top the weirdness factor then she didn't want to know what did.

It is possible. To a point.

That's good to know, she said. *At least I'm going to have some benefits while you are visiting.*

There are many.

That peaked her curiosity. *Like what?*

You have access to my knowledge. As I have access to yours.

Her eyebrows shot up at that. *Really?* She couldn't resist peeking. She found his memories, like a vast room behind a door in her mind, and cast her thoughts back to the Broken One's earliest memories as a young boy. She'd thought he was male, but hadn't known for sure. She wondered if any female souls had been bonded to styluses.

The answer came immediately to her from…somewhere inside. No. Only males were allowed to bond.

That was hardly fair.

The Broken One said, *It has been that way, always. The Torans don't have females in power positions. They wouldn't allow Louers to have them either.*

Right. That made sense. She didn't like it, but it was logical. Women had some power in her world, but—

Not in all areas. I see much of your dimension is split on that issue.

She sighed. *Yes that is true. In many parts of the world, women are considered property and nothing more.*

There are many problems in your dimension.

She knew it couldn't be physical, but she felt a spidery, crawling sensation as the Broken One accessed her memories. She couldn't blame him. He was big on knowledge and she'd opened that door herself. There was such a duality to the moment. She had access to great knowledge, but there was also a hesitation to share her own. It was…private.

She almost laughed. Nothing would be private any more. The Broken One could see and experience everything in her life. As she could his. It wasn't intrusive, or jarring, just…odd? Maybe. She didn't know how to express it.

While she floundered to name her cascading feelings, a familiar face loomed close to her. Eric. She smiled. "Hey. I'm okay."

"You don't look it."

If his expression was anything to go by, she must look awful. His brows had pulled together into a dark vee and the angles of his face had hardened with worry. Even his lips were pressed firmly together. And the color, she didn't know if it was the foggy atmosphere, but his skin had taken on a gray pallor. Had she scared him that badly?

He snatched her up and hugged her tight.

She burrowed deeper into his arms. "Sorry," she murmured. "This is all so strange."

"Is that what you call it?" His attempt at humor fell flat. "Honestly, this is painful for me. I can't do anything, but watch." He squeezed her, then settled back a bit and stroked her back. He sighed, a deep welling release that she felt in her own body.

"I'm so sorry. This isn't how I'd planned to escape In-between."

He gave a gurgling laugh. She reared back to look at him. Was he crying? No. More of a choking laugh.

"I'm glad you had a plan. It would have helped to be filled in on it." He smiled. "Only you could call this mess a plan."

She moaned. "I know. I so have to work on that."

He smiled down at her. "You are one crazy girl. Now…do you have any idea what's next? I know I keep pushing the idea of leaving here, but I really want to go home."

"The styluses said that they need to recuperate from transferring the Broken One to me."

He peered down at her. "How long?"

She frowned. "I have no idea."

He closed his eyes and dropped his head. "Right. More waiting. And in this case, it could be a long time."

The Broken One spoke through Storey. "We can move now. The bond between you and your stylus is strong. We still need to wait for our power to regenerate for the next step, but we can do that in another dimension."

Storey brightened. *Really?*

"Yes."

Eric hopped to his feet, and carefully tugged Storey upwards. "Good. Let's go. I vote to go back to my dimension."

The Broken One spoke again, "That is not possible."

Eric froze. "And why is that?"

"In order to leave this dimension, Storey has to feel a strong bond to somewhere. Her bond to your dimension is tainted by your father. It would be hard to use that energy to successfully port home. However, she has a strong bond to her dimension that we could, possibly, build on."

That made sense and for all that she was sorry, the Broken One's assessment of Eric's dimension was true. She did have a negative feeling about that place and all because of the Councilman. Not a fair attitude and one she'd get over, but since her current predicament was because of him…

"Why can't we just port out?" Eric asked. "Now that you are here and functioning, and we have the coordinates of this place – point of origin – so to speak, why can't we just leave? Dillon did."

Storey wanted to hear that answer herself.

"Dillon didn't port out. Dillon's soul ported out."

Oh shit.

ERIC'S STOMACH HEAVED. Would this never be over? Whatever happened to an honest battle? He could handle that. Death, under those circumstances, was also understandable. He'd always known that every time he left his dimension in his capacity as a Ranger, he might never return.

This half world where neither life nor death existed was painful. He wanted to hit out at something and he couldn't even get into a decent argument with the stylus as it was ultimately Storey he'd be arguing with and that wouldn't work. He wanted to protect her – not hurt her.

And what he really wanted was to get them both out of

this hell hole. This stylus deal had become so much bigger. What they'd just done with the Broken One…well, he couldn't begin to explain. But he'd kept the broken stylus just in case they'd need it down the road. As he'd come to realize, nothing was ever finished.

"What do we need to get out of here once and for all? Intact. As in our bodies leaving with us."

Storey rolled her eyes at him. A quirky grin spread across her face. A lightness that only happened when she was around swelled inside. She could do that to him. Only her. Make a dark day lighter, sweeter. Just by being there. There was a special connection he always felt around her. A sense that it was just the two of them. That they were aligned against the rest of the world.

He relaxed. "I'm not trying to be pushy here. But I want a solution that keeps us alive and well, thank you."

At that Storey laughed. "Me too."

"Broken One?" he asked. "Have you a way out of this dimension?"

"We think so."

Storey lifted a brow as her mouth moved, but a different voice spoke.

Eric shook his head. It was so weird for him to see her, but hear the Broken One. That the stylus's voice was rougher, raspier, helped him to identify the speaker, but he couldn't imagine how Storey felt to have another soul inside using her vocal cords, her body.

"And what is that?"

Eric waited, hoping that the answer would be easy. He'd had enough of these puzzles that only seemed to embroil them all further.

"We need to have a strong energy connection that would

allow us to build a portal to the other side. Storey's ability to draw would be instrumental in this. But she needs to feel very strongly about something in order for that energy, that caring, to be powerful enough for us to utilize the energy to power the process."

"Like my mother!" Storey laughed. "I so want to see her again. To be home again."

"Yes, that was our impression."

Eric waited, there was a 'but'…in there somewhere.

An uncomfortable silence filled the fog.

CHAPTER 11

"BROKEN ONE? IS there a problem?" Storey frowned. Her voice changed, deepened, as he said, "Your mother. There are some issues there. A time element that makes it difficult."

She groaned. Now that home had been mentioned as the ideal option, she couldn't stop the yearning inside to return to her own dimension. "Do what we have to do to get out of here."

"That might not be an ideal location with our limited power. Even with your strong feelings."

She closed her eyes and worked on bolstering her diminishing patience. "Then what is?"

"Someone else you care for, enough for us to build on the energy."

Her gaze flew to Eric. "Someone else is Eric. But he's here with us."

"Building a portal to him means a portal to here," said the Broken One. "Of no value."

She rolled her eyes. "Was that an attempt at humor?"

"We are learning. You have much laughter in your memories. Much joy. We would like to experience that."

"Don't you remember laughing?" As the question left her lips, she was bombarded with memories of his childhood. Sober, sad, alone with other slaves and working as he was given work to do. The life of a child slave hadn't been much fun. Although there were some times that were more lighthearted, she couldn't see any instances of real joy. There were no rocks being kicked around in a game, or running in sunlight just for fun. There were only solemn instances of work, discussion, aloneness and…not a hug in there.

"Were you abused?" She didn't think so, but…

"Not by your definition."

"Loved?"

"Not by your definition."

"Loving relationships? What about your mother? Father? Siblings? Friends? Lovers?"

"No."

His thoughts were clear, curious, detached. He had no experience with relationships. At all.

"Not true."

Right – he could read her mind. How weird was it that they were reading each other's minds, but were both speaking aloud using her vocal cords so as to include Eric in the discussion.

"I have a strong relationship with my community."

She smiled slowly, and inside her that sense of connectedness brightened. It was a strong, caring bond and she was glad he'd had that much. In fact, it was more than many people experienced in her own dimension.

"That is possible. I am not unhappy with my existence." He made an odd sound. "Especially now that you have saved it."

"And you are very welcome for that," she said sincerely. "Now I hope you can help me regain my life."

"We do too." He was silent for a long moment. "You need someone else you are connected to. Preferably someone where your feelings are still strong today. Not a relationship from a long time ago."

No one came to mind. She didn't know what to say. Who did she care about? Her mother, Eric, a few school friends. She had no siblings or nieces and nephews…she gasped. "Tammy!"

Eric looked at her in surprise. "You do really miss her, don't you?"

"I do and…" she emphasized, her voice rising. "Remember, I said she was trying to communicate telepathically with me? There is that bond as well."

"Will that be enough?"

The Broken One stepped in and said, "There is much affection for her. That is good."

"Is it?" Storey asked. "We can't see each other. I can't communicate with her and even though she's back home again where she belongs, I miss her."

"It's dangerous for us to go there." Eric groaned. "But it's still better than being here."

"And that is the emotional energy we can use to leave this place."

Storey paced a small circle. "What can I do to help?"

"And me?" Eric said. "There has to be some way we can both help."

Storey heard the answer like a faint echo in her mind. The two styluses were talking, but so low she couldn't understand the conversation. "They're busy doing something. I can barely hear them."

Eric squatted down slightly and pulled out one of his packs, expanding it. "I have your sketchbooks here. Maybe you can do something with them."

Storey squatted beside him. "I don't suppose you have

anything to eat in there, do you?"

Eric laughed as his hand found the block of cheese he'd pulled from her house. He lifted it free and waved it around in front of her. She gasped in delight, but instead of going after the cheese, she dove into his pack. "What else have you got hidden in here?"

She found the granola bar within minutes. "Yes!" She unwrapped and bit into it immediately.

The look in his eyes made her stop. She held it out to him. "Sorry, do you want a bite?"

"Go ahead." He shook his head and chuckled. "You need it more than I do."

Storey broke the bar in half and handed over the second piece. "Here. We both need our strength." He took it with a smile and popped the whole thing in his mouth.

She shook her head. She'd seen her male school friends eat like that. It always amazed her. How could so much fit in one mouth? But he wasn't worried about choking. He'd already pulled out his knife and was slicing chunks of cheese into her hand. Greedily she popped the largest one into her mouth. "Any chance there's an apple in there?"

Eric nodded. "Maybe the Broken One should use your love of food to mine the emotional energy they need. They could create a portal to your mother's kitchen."

She grinned. "I love it. It should be a cakewalk to mine a path to Tammy. Hell, if she knew I had this food, she'd be coming here to find us!" The smile fell away and she chewed very slowly. Both on the cheese and the worrisome thought in her mind.

"What?" Eric raised a brow at her as he popped more cheese into his mouth.

She swallowed the last of her mouthful, then stared at

the slices in her hand. "Does this mean we're going to Tammy? And the rest of the Louers? The ones that held us prisoner last time?" She looked at him, knowing her fatigue and fear had to be showing. "They hate us. I'm not sure I can deal with all that again."

He reached out and grabbed her shoulder. "You can do it. At least there, we know what the problem is. What the solution is."

She nodded. "I'm just tired. I can draw a portal and use it to escape as soon as we arrive."

"Why not do that now? We may not have much prep time before the Broken One has things ready." He pulled the sketchbook forward and handed it over.

Reinvigorated, she shoved the last of her piece of cheese into her mouth, wiped her hands on her jeans and reached for the book. She frowned at it. "Where did you get this?"

"From your room."

"I don't have any like this in my room. This is smooth paper. Silky. I prefer a rougher texture." She shrugged, not wanting to delve too deeply into why this book would be in her room. "Whatever."

She pulled her stylus free from around her neck. Opening to a blank page, she closed her eyes and asked her stylus, *What do I need to draw? Portals? Or Tammy's face?*

Her head started to vibrate inside. She squeezed her eyes shut, afraid her brain was going to bounce off the inside of her skull. A shudder drummed its way down her spine.

Stop it. That hurts.

The pounding in her head ceased. She took a shaky breath. *Thank you.*

We must work. It would be better if you slept.

I can't just sleep. I'm not tired. Well I am, but I can't just go to sleep when I want.

Yes you can.

Storey smiled. *It's not that ea—*

She fell to the floor. Asleep.

"STOREY? STOREY, WHAT'S wrong?" Eric knelt beside Storey. She breathed easily, her color remained normal. He reached a hand to her forehead. Reassured that she was in fact still alive, he settled back on his heels to wait.

"Damn it, Storey. What the hell do I do now?"

Of course no one answered. Typical. But he could talk to Paxton. He quickly sent a message, bringing Paxton up to date. And asked about the status of Dillon.

He read the response out loud. "No information on Dillon. Why is she sleeping?" He snorted. "As if I know. And I'd like to."

He reached over again and stroked her hair back off her forehead. Surely this wasn't a normal sleep. She lay as if dead, not even shuffling or rolling over. She slept as if she hadn't seen sleep in days. Sure, she was exhausted, but this…it wasn't normal. He could only hope this place wasn't affecting her like it had Dillon.

All he could do was stand guard over her.

But for how long?

He waited and waited. And waited.

CHAPTER 12

S TOREY CAME AWAKE slowly. She opened her eyes and saw Eric sitting at her side. She had no recollection of falling asleep, yet she felt…rested. And depressed. She was still in In-between. Grey fog totally encompassed the two of them. Damn.

Her head was full. Her thoughts had some clarity though, as if the rest had been what she'd needed. She sat up slowly, happy to see there was no residual headache. That pain had been crippling. "Eric?"

He leaned toward her, his smile a bright light in the gloomy atmosphere. "Hi. Enjoy your nap?"

She winced. "I'd have enjoyed it more if I'd woken up in one of the other dimensions."

"You and me both," Eric said with a groan.

Feeling good, she could sympathize. "And that wasn't sleep as much as enforced rest." She explained what the Broken One had done.

His mouth formed a big O. "What? He knocked you out without your permission?"

She winced. "Permission is a difficult thing when you're sharing a body."

"You're not sharing. He's a guest. Remember that."

She struggled to her feet. "I'm trying to. And if I'm awake, I'm going to assume that he's done whatever they needed to do. Maybe," she glanced around, "we can leave now."

Eric stayed sitting. "I hope so. But I doubt it. Nothing is going as planned this trip," he said gloomily.

She laughed, reached a hand down, waiting until he grasped hers, and helped him stand up. "Are you trying to tell me that you actually *had* a plan this time?"

He grinned modestly. "Hey, I thought we could wing it. We've done that a time or two before."

She went to say something when a shutter blanked the words from her mind and the Broken One spoke using her vocal cords, his gravelly voice surprisingly deep. "It is time."

Eric shouted, "Yes!"

Storey was a little less enthused. She wanted to hear the details first. She asked, her voice surprisingly normal, "Broken One. Where are we going? And how are we travelling?"

"To Tammy's home. By your portal drawings."

Eric's brows shot up in surprise. "Tammy's dimension? Is that safe?"

"It doesn't matter. It is the only option."

Storey spluttered. It didn't matter? Is so mattered. His next word stopped her in her tracks.

"Tammy is waiting for you," the Broken One said.

She gasped in joy. She'd forgotten that the styluses could communicate telepathically with the Louers. Something about their combined abilities, adaptability and technological advancement. "You spoke with her? How is she?"

"She is well."

Eric said, "I still don't get this telepathic stuff."

"It is only language. And using energy as the translator."

With a shake of his head, Eric said, "I wanted to ask – is Dillon the first Toran to be soul bound to a stylus?"

"No."

Storey remembered Eric hadn't been in on the earlier conversation. He didn't know what Dillon was.

The Broken One added, "Dillon is not a Toran. He is a Louer."

She gasped, finally realizing what she'd missed earlier. She stared up at Eric.

Eric frowned down at her, obviously not understanding.

She didn't know if he hadn't put the dots together or if the connected dots really didn't matter. Cautiously, she said, "I didn't realize you have Torans and Louers intermingled in your Toran dimension. I'd assumed all the Louers had been banished."

He shrugged. "They were."

Storey sucked in her breath. And waited.

Eric shook his head. "I'm not dense, but the way you're looking at me, as if I'm missing something important, is making me feel that way."

She took a deep breath and hoped she didn't have to explain.

"Oh, hell." Eric shared at her stunned.

Yeah, he got it. Finally. He narrowed his gaze. "You're saying Dillon is a Louer. And he was in the Toran dimension. So therefore at one time, they were mingling."

"Dillon wasn't a slave."

"I remember that, too."

"And," she prompted.

He frowned. "And what?" His expression cleared as he finally understood what she'd been getting at. Then a thundercloud swept across his face. "It can't be. There has to be some mistake."

"I don't think there is."

"It's not possible. Paxton is Dillon's brother. If Dillon is a Louer, that means our top philosopher, our greatest scientific leader, the confidant of our Council and the eldest of all the council members – is a Louer."

Now he got it.

ERIC COULDN'T THINK. The facts, as he understood them, swirled into a dark, chaotic form that made no sense to his brain. Was it possible that Paxton was a Louer? Dillon looked like the same race as Eric or Storey, but then from what Eric had learned from her and the styluses about his people's history, Dillon would. The Louers' appearance had changed over time due to hardship – a hardship that Dillon…and Paxton…had missed. It boggled the mind.

How could it have happened?

"In all societies that employ slavery, some slaves hold higher positions than others. It's quite possible that Paxton's parents or grandparents were free people." Storey suggested, her tone quiet. "Maybe they had migrated from Louers to Torans and no one knew."

"It could change everything at home."

"If anyone finds out." She shrugged her shoulders. "I won't tell."

It wasn't that easy. Eric had no idea how he should feel. His mentor, the man he preferred to think of as his best friend, perhaps even as a father, was the enemy.

As if reading his thoughts, Storey said, "Just don't make the mistake of thinking that Paxton and Dillon are the enemy. Paxton has shown by his every action that he is as much a Toran as you."

Eric nodded. "I understand that."

"But?" Storey narrowed her eyes at him. "It makes no

difference. You might want to also consider that given how long ago this could have happened, that Paxton might not even know."

Shocked, Eric studied her features. "How could that be? Of course he'd know."

"First off, his own parents might not have known. If they didn't, then he wouldn't have. It's not something you'd speak about normally. And even if he did know, Paxton has devoted his very long life to serving the Torans. He's kept you safe and helped in every way he could. You can't blame him for this."

"I'm not blaming him," Eric said slowly, "But there is a sense of betrayal."

That garnered him a dismissive look. "For not having told you? How could he? Especially once all the problems started. If he knows, he'd have to wait for the right time to tell you. And understand – there is no good time for bad news."

Eric didn't want to discuss it anymore. He couldn't. He had no idea of how to feel and certainly wasn't going to hash out the issue right now. He shoved it all away and tried to refocus. "The Broken One says it's time to go. Let's deal with that first. There will be plenty of time later to talk to Paxton."

Storey gave him a slow nod. "True. You and Paxton need some time alone to discuss this. Your father is already a big issue in your life. You don't want to do anything that would put a rift in your relationship with Paxton, too."

She was right. He knew that. Even the thought of losing Paxton brought a pang to his heart. But later. He'd deal with that later. Firmly, he said, "Let's get out of *this* mess first."

CHAPTER 13

WATCHING THE CONFUSION and turmoil on Eric's face, Storey realized how much she'd come to care for many of the Torans – especially Eric. He was special. And she'd even developed a kinship to Paxton. He was the only other person who'd bonded to a stylus that she knew of, after all.

Broken One, can we proceed?

Yes. Draw Tammy in her home. Make her happy and glad to see you. Connect emotionally.

That wouldn't be hard. Tammy had always been happy to see Storey. She'd been taken captive by a party of her own people hoping to force her father to take them home. Storey had saved her.

She picked up her stylus, and sank into the memory. There'd been such a glow in the girl's eyes when she'd realized she hadn't been deserted. That someone cared enough to help her. She's been so despondent before that, the contrast on her face had been emblazoned on Storey's memory. With that picture of hope, of joy, she overlaid the last glimpse she'd had of Tammy as her father walked away with her in his arms.

Her hand moved, slowly at first, carefully laying the picture down as she had it in her mind. Then she picked up speed. The stylus moved with such finesse and such accuracy, she knew she couldn't be doing it on her own. In fact, she'd have to admit this drawing was stronger, and more powerful than anything she'd done before.

Was that the addition of the Broken One?

Yes. We are one.

Stylus, this is only a picture of Tammy, don't I need to draw a portal as well?

We are doing that at the same time, her stylus said. The comforting sound of her own stylus made her sigh happily. Their connection was more than just instrument and operator. She'd like the think the sense of familiarity she had with her stylus was the beginning of friendship. She'd fought to keep her stylus. And even now couldn't begin to imagine life without it. Him. Them. She shrugged. She understood they were a collective of souls, but since she heard them as one voice, she thought of it as him. Right or wrong.

Of course being soul bound, if they were separated, she'd die.

Thank you.

She stilled. *For what?*

For feeling the sense of connection that has been missing in our world. As we have bonded to the stylus, we have also bonded to you. And you to us. That makes our relationship more than it has been before. It makes us whole.

But you were bonded to a scientist before, correct?

Correct. We bonded to him for our existence, but he did not bond to us.

Ah, she said. *So no mental, or emotional connection.*

Or respect.

She pursed her lips at that.

"Storey? Are you even watching what you are doing?"

She glanced over at Eric to see him staring at her in confusion. She blinked and looked down at her picture. She'd drawn a photographic image of Tammy in a dwelling of some kind. Her arms were open as if waiting for a hug and the smile on her face tugged at Storey's heart. She barely heard her own happy gasp at the look of joy in Tammy's eyes. The picture was stunning in its detail. And still her hand flashed and darted, adding a line here, a shadow there.

"I so want to keep this after we are done." She said. She stared at the warmth in Tammy's eyes. And saw, tucked into Tammy's hair, was her pet, Skorky. Storey chuckled. She'd even be happy to see the rat-like critter again.

"It's stunning, but look, you've got a door in front of her, one we can walk through. Except it's so small and the paper itself is small…how is this going to work?" Eric's tone was exasperated. Doubt twisted his lips as he shook his head. "This can't work. We've always had a piece of paper large enough to step into. Drawn the way you have it, it's a door like you did in Paxton's lab that first time, only you did it so it appeared at the end of a hallway. Like a perspective drawing."

"We can always use more paper," she suggested.

Not necessary. This is functional.

Storey lifted her eyebrow and repeated the stylus's words to Eric.

He turned to study the drawing in progress. Then got up, walked behind her and stared down over her shoulder. "Really?" he muttered. "If you say so. Then can we go? This damn place is starting to give me the creeps."

Storey almost laughed at hearing her thoughts coming out of his mouth. But he wouldn't appreciate it at this time. Or any time.

Then her hand stopped moving. Such an abrupt halt it

startled her. She wondered if she could ever do art on her own ever again. With the stylus having become such a creative force behind her drawings, she'd never know what was her art and what was *their* art.

You will know.

Maybe. It wasn't the issue right now. She turned her attention to the sketchpad. She understood what Eric was saying. It didn't look big enough to be of use. Then this wasn't exactly a normal dimension.

Exactly.

"So how do we make this work?" She stood up. She held the picture out in front so both she and Eric could study it.

"Tammy looks so happy to see us, doesn't she?" And that made Storey anxious to see her. That little girl was special.

"Keep in mind – this is a drawing. The stylus can make her look as it wants her to look. That doesn't make it real. Or correct."

Ah, Eric's pragmatic approach to life. "Then let's find out."

"How?"

The stylus was silent.

Hmmm. Storey studied the picture. She looked up at Eric. "I think they're expecting us to know what to do with this."

He snorted. "Like that's going to happen." He waved an arm around. "We can't do anything here."

That wasn't quite true. They could do a lot. They just had to think differently. She created the rules here…somewhat. She wondered…could it be that easy? She remembered back to when she'd first arrived, and finding how falling and stopping worked, that so much of it was done by mental control. So if the perspective was the issue, then could she pin this paper to…the fog…and have it hang there?

Holding the paper gently, she detached it from the book and giving Eric a reassuring smile, she mentally, and physically, pinned the picture to the wall of fog.

It stayed there.

She grinned and stepped back. "There."

"Well it's hanging, but so what?"

As she studied the painting, she had to laugh. Unbelievable. Being a couple of feet in front of her, the fog had moved in, sliding a slight veil around the picture.

Giving it a distance. A perspective.

"Take another look at it."

Eric planted his hands on his hips and stared at the picture. She stared at him. And watched as he saw it. "The atmosphere here is making the perspective happen as if the picture is real and the fog is real."

"Right, we're approaching Tammy's home in deep fog conditions and look, there's a light in the picture."

He gave a short bark of a laugh. "So we just walk forward?"

"I'm guessing so."

She reached out for his hand. He clasped hers in his much larger one. Together they walked the short distance to the door. As they arrived, the door in the picture opened.

And they walked through.

ERIC COULDN'T HELP holding his breath as they entered the drawing. But just as with all the other strange portals Storey and her stylus had created, he stepped into a whole new world.

And a familiar sound had him dropping Storey's hand to clap both palms over his ears. He groaned, barely hearing Storey call out, "Tammy, hush. It's me, Storey."

The sound cut off instantly. Tammy's eyes widened. Then she launched herself from where she'd been sitting at Eric and Storey.

Eric, knowing the size of the bomb about to blast them, tried to brace himself, but she knocked him back several steps, while they both knocked Storey over.

Storey cried out, then all Eric heard was her laughter. He disentangled himself from Tammy's legs and turned. He grinned. Storey was lying down and Tammy almost eclipsed her as she lay on top. Skorky raced over and around both of them, getting in the way as they laughed. Storey was tickling the chubby little Louer who wiggled frantically to get away, but at the same time, obviously didn't want to go anywhere.

"Torrey."

Storey, her grin splitting her face almost in two, hugged her close. Skorky dashed over Storey's head to take up residence on Tammy's shoulder, his beady eyes bright and curious. Tammy's over-bright eyes looked up at Eric. She sniffled happily. Something warm and fuzzy bloomed in Eric's heart. He'd never felt anything like it. At this moment, he couldn't be happier. They were in danger, had just survived what could have been an endless hell, yet seeing Storey and Tammy together made up for all of it.

He'd never thought to see Tammy again. Hadn't given any energy to wishing that any different. Now that he saw her, and her connection to Storey, he realized how much he'd missed the little girl himself. He'd just shut those emotions down, believing that a relationship wasn't possible.

Then Tammy scrambled to her feet and wrapped her arms around him. He hugged her tight.

Once again his world had shifted. Thanks to Storey.

Chapter 14

S TOREY FINALLY MANAGED to clamber to her feet. She took several deep breaths and rejoiced. They were free from In-between and they'd successfully reached Tammy. As Tammy and Eric enjoyed their reunion, she glanced around at Tammy's small room. Dirt walls again. Maybe that's all her people knew.

Or maybe that's all they'd been able to achieve so far. But Tammy appeared to have a bed, something like a small table and there'd been an attempt made to carve shelves into one wall. With Tammy's few things, like Storey's bag, she'd made the little room look like home.

On one wall were scratch drawings. Tammy's artwork, she presumed, studying the stick men in the picture. She walked closer. A small hand snuck into hers. Tammy reached out with her other hand and tapped the wall with the artwork.

Skorky ran across Tammy's arm to jump on a ledge and stare at them.

"Torrey." She tapped the wall and one skinny stick figure. Tammy grinned up at her. Storey was entranced. For the whole time she'd looked after Tammy, the child had shown little to no facial expressions. As if their race didn't use them. Over time, Tammy had learned to mimic more of the expressions she'd seen on Eric and Storey.

But this appeared to be her first spontaneous grin.

And it was beautiful. Storey bent, hugged the little girl, and said, "Thank you Tammy."

"Storey, do you think you can communicate with her again? Now that the styluses apparently contacted her?"

"I don't know." She straightened. "Tammy, do you know how to communicate with me, now?"

No response. She closed her eyes. *Stylus. Can you help me to communicate with Tammy?*

Don't need help. Tammy here.

Storey gasped and opened her eyes. She shared a special smile with Tammy, then turned to face Eric, excitement and that wonderful sense of connection flowing through her. "Tammy is here and we can communicate!"

"Telepathically, of course. Which means I'm only going to be able to get half the conversation again." He rolled his eyes in exaggeration, but his smile eased any sting.

She smiled back at him. "I'm sorry for that. Maybe you can learn to communicate telepathically as well."

Torrey?

Storey turned back to Tammy. *Yes?*

Are you in trouble?

Storey groaned loudly, but kept a smile on her face. *We are. This time you helped save us!*

Tammy danced several steps. Then her steps slowed as if understanding what would come next. *Are you leaving again?*

Soon. I need to return to my home first. Then come back here for another quick visit. Maybe if we can talk this way now, we can talk once I return home, too.

Tammy's face lit up.

"What brought that on?" Eric asked.

Storey laughed, holding out her hand to Tammy. "I was

telling her that now we might be able to keep in touch."

"Do you think that would work across dimensions?" Eric frowned. "If that's the case, I might have to try to learn. Then we could stay in touch all the time."

"And if that doesn't work, you could get me a codex that allows me to write messages like you've been doing with Paxton. It wouldn't be as good as telepathy, but we would be in constant contact. Instead of planning visits." She chuckled. "Or better yet – you should get a stylus of your own."

"That's not likely to happen." He pulled up his codex and considered it. "I think both of these have that ability." He lifted her wrist, reminding her that she wore one already. "We'll test it later. First, are we going back to Paxton's lab or to your home world? As much as Tammy is happy to see us, I'm not so sure about her father."

Right. The leader of the Louers, Tammy's father, had knocked them out with their nasty telepathic weapon the last time they'd seen him. The horrible noise that made an unconscious state actually preferable.

She glanced down at Tammy. *Tammy does your father know we are here?*

She nodded. Storey gasped. *Did he know ahead of time? No.*

So how does he know now?

Tammy cocked her head and frowned up at Storey in confusion. *He can hear us, of course.*

"Oh shit." Storey turned to Eric. "Her father apparently can hear this telepathic conversation so he knows we're here."

Eric immediately started punching coordinates that he'd used not too long ago to take him to Storey's dimension. "Tell her we have to go. We can't get into trouble with her father again."

As Storey relayed the message, Tammy's face crumpled.

"Ah Eric, we need to leave now. She looks like she's going to start crying."

"Hold her off," he said, urgently desperate to stop that horrible shrill sound of hell that would soon be coming out of Tammy's mouth. Then his codex started its musical notes, instantly distracting Tammy. The little girl reached out to touch the flashing lights.

"Whoa." Eric backed up. "Storey, get over here."

She quickly stepped right beside him as the black smoke rose up around his legs. She waved goodbye to Tammy, saying. *We'll be back soon, honey.*

Tammy's eyes filled with tears. She launched herself at Storey.

And the black mist closed around them all.

"STOREY, PLEASE TELL me that didn't just happen?"

Silence.

"Storey," he snapped. "Talk to me."

"I'm here. But so is Tammy." She added humorously, "I guess our visit wasn't long enough."

"Damn it." He couldn't believe it. Why did everything go wrong? This should have been so simple – get in and get out. No one should have even noticed.

A choked giggle slipped from Storey.

Short arms reached around his waist and Tammy snuggled close.

He glared into the mist, then sighed and wrapped an arm around Tammy's back. He reached out and tugged Storey in closer where he could see her face. "What are you laughing at?"

"You." She added, "You swore."

"Did not." But he had. And she knew it. Drat. She just smiled up at him. He'd always liked that about her. She never judged him. No matter what.

"What do we do now?" she asked.

"If her father finds out she came with us, there goes any chance of a peaceful relationship."

"Speaking of which, I'm thinking the stylus needs to contact Tammy's father and explain what happened."

He stared at. "If it can do that, why didn't it do it before?"

She shrugged. "Maybe it did."

We did not. We can.

Then please do so. It's our intention to return Tammy immediately.

A buzz filled the air.

"Uh, Storey?"

She wrapped her arm around him. "It's okay. It's the stylus doing something."

"That's what worries me!" Tammy's round face peered up at him through the gloom. She smiled, her empty hand reaching up to pat his cheek. "Ris."

"Eric." Eric covered her hand with his. "Eric. Try it again."

"Riss."

"I'm going to presume hard sounds like Ks aren't easy for her."

Storey giggled. "And what's her problem with E?"

The mist started to dissipate. A wave of relief washed through him. Maybe something would go right for a change.

The sun twinkled brightly overhead and green trees surrounded them.

Tammy's eye shone as she looked around with the mist almost gone.

Eric said, "Looks like she recognizes the area. You can almost see the look in her eyes, saying food is around the corner."

At that Storey laughed again. "And she's welcome to it. I have never met anyone with an appetite like hers."

"Good thing she doesn't know about the rest of the cheese in my bag," he said smugly.

"Let's hang on to it. We might need your supplies for later." Storey headed off in the direction of her home.

Tammy followed, her hand securely held in Eric's.

Eric gave a last glance into the bushes around them and followed.

What would they find this time?

CHAPTER 15

S TOREY TILTED HER face to the sun. What day was it?
The sun appeared to be high in the sky. If it was a
weekday, then she might be lucky enough to find the house
empty. If it was a weekend, then one…or both…of her
parents could be there. And she so didn't want to meet them.
Not in this time. Her mother, if things were back to normal…yes. She wanted to hug her tight and tell her how
much she loved her.

But if it was the crazy life where she went to a private
religious school and her father, who she hadn't seen in a
decade, was home and still married to her mother, no way.
Like how weird…and wrong…was that?

She admitted to being ambivalent on many of the issues,
but she really didn't want to live the other Storey's life. That
one did her schoolwork and never picked up an art pencil.
This Storey would die under those conditions. Her art was
her outlet. Her path to freedom from the world around her.
She *had* to be able to draw.

And she would, no matter what. If what Eric had said
was true about her room being full of art books she didn't
recognize, then maybe the other Storey had already learned
she needed to draw.

Maybe there was crossover, or bleeding from one Storey
to the other. Time had twisted, but what else had twisted

with it?

She reached the end of the trees and stopped. Her home stood in front of her. Its familiar clapboard siding stirred pangs of homesickness inside. She desperately wanted to see her mother. The real one. Not the other one. Storey sighed. How did life get so confused?

Tammy tugged on her hand. Storey looked down at her trusting face, wondering at the child's sympathetic look. There was no way Tammy could really understand what bothered Storey at this time. But Tammy was offering what comfort she could.

And Storey was happy to accept it.

She smiled down at Tammy. "Let's go."

Tammy's smile kicked up a notch. They approached from the side. Storey led the way to the back kitchen door. She cautiously walked up the few stairs to the porch and tried the door. Locked. Damn. She left Tammy in Eric's care then slipped around the side of the house to the garage. There she crept into inside, relieved to find it empty. She crossed over to the inside door and found it locked too.

Rolling her eyes at fate, she whispered out loud, "You'd think there had been a series of break-ins where people raided the refrigerator or something."

Her mother had always kept a spare key under the freezer. She walked over to find the old chest freezer locked. But the spare key was still in the same old place. Gleefully, she picked up the key and unlocked the house door. She walked in cautiously. She couldn't be sure no one was home. At first glance the place seemed empty and that made her relax – slightly. Walking through the kitchen she unlocked the back door and let Eric and Tammy in. "Go on upstairs."

"What are you going to do?" Eric asked, already ushering

Tammy ahead of him toward the stairs.

She rolled her eyes at him. "Look for food of course. What else?" She turned to the fridge. After all the times they'd raided this thing she wouldn't be surprised to find a lock on it. Not this time though. She studied the contents and realized there wasn't much that was grab and go. The kind of food she could offer without cooking it first. She did find a couple of oranges. In the pantry was a box of cookies and a box of snack crackers. She took both of those.

The problem was, Tammy could be expecting a mess of other food. She searched back in the fridge, but there was no meat that she could take up. She rummaged through the other cupboards and found an unopened package of beef jerky. Then she hit the motherload – a large box of Halloween mini-sized chocolate bars.

Perfect. Tammy wasn't going to argue with those. Not once she tried them.

She made a swift circle through the downstairs, recognizing the furniture as being the same from her last visit. On the mantle, a family photo. With all three of them together. That meant her father was still in this life. With that confirmation, she ran up the stairs to her room. At the door, she stopped. Took a deep breath and kicked it lightly. Eric opened it immediately. His eyes lit up at her armload.

"Here let me help."

"No, it's okay. I'll just dump it all on the bed." She did just that. Tammy came running and jumped up beside the pile. Her chunky fingers immediately reached for the closest item. Storey snatched the orange back just before she bit into the rind. She tossed it to Eric. "This has to be peeled or cut into quarters."

She kept a wary eye on Tammy's face. Her mouth in a

shocked O, then it crumpled. "Oh shit." Storey opened the box of snack crackers and pulled out several for her. She took the first one and popped it into her mouth. Tammy took several and shoved them into hers.

"Well, that much hasn't changed at least." Storey backed up several steps and turned to Eric. He was turning the orange over and over in his hands. She sighed. "Here give me that. I'll peel it." And she did, quickly and efficiently. Within minutes she split it into two halves and handed over both to the two people staring at her like she was going to be their next meal.

Eric bit into his half and his eyes grew rounder. He chewed, then bit again. "It's good!"

Tammy, after seeing Eric, shoved as much of the orange into her mouth as she could. Storey peeled the second orange. Then showing the two of them, broke it into sections and popped one section into her mouth and chewed it. Then popped a second one in. She split the rest into pieces for both the others. They followed her example and ate it slowly.

Storey left the two working their way through the food and went to the bathroom. She groaned at the picture in the mirror. Instead of things getting better, she was starting to look haggard. In-between obviously hadn't done anything good for her. She knew that when she closed her eyes to sleep, she was more than likely to have horrible nightmares of being caught In-between. Forever.

That type of fear would stay with her for a long time.

As would the 'what ifs' that kept going through her mind. What if Eric hadn't come for her? What if she hadn't found the Broken One in the Louers' dimension? What if she couldn't fix her own dimension…and things never went back the way they were supposed to be?

We can fix it. But we need time…and trust.

Thank you. Hot tears filled her eyes. She closed them, willing them not to fall. She needed to stay strong. Her stylus was right. They could fix this. She'd fixed so much that surely this was the last big one to handle.

She just needed to get it right. She was no longer alone with this burden. Surely it would be easier with the Broken One to help. She smiled. Grabbing a washcloth, she scrubbed her hands and face.

And noticed the honor marks. Intricate golden scrolls across her collarbone and down her arm. Surely there were more now than before. So faint as to not be noticed on first glance, but now that she could see them… She rinsed her washcloth and stroked warm water over them. They warmed to the touch. She smiled.

They looked good. Great in fact. Mysterious and yet subtle.

She liked them.

Good. We are glad.

She took an extra few minutes, grabbed a brush and tugged the knots out of her hair. Refreshed, she headed back to the others.

She *was* hungry. A bite first, then she needed to get to work.

She wanted her life back.

"UM, STOREY, I appreciate the food. Honest. But I thought the plan was to turn around and send Tammy back. Immediately." He studied the strip of dark brown hard stuff. Odd. But he was game. He hadn't had anything from her yet that wasn't good. He really hoped to keep the cheese to take back to his dimension. That stuff was addictive.

She looked at him in surprise. Then grabbed a few crackers and stuffed them her mouth. He studied her for a long moment. "You don't want to send her back right away, do you?" A wave of bright pink washed up her face. He settled back. He understood, but they couldn't allow her affection for Tammy get in the way of what they needed to do.

With a telltale sigh, Storey dropped her gaze to Tammy's face and sighed. "She's special."

"Yes, she is." He waited.

Storey glanced over at him sheepishly. "It's just for a little while. How long are we here for? A half hour? An hour maybe. Then we have to go back anyway. I really want to fix my home before anything else goes wrong. And remember what the styluses, or was it Paxton, said? I can't remember who. Anyway, they said increased traffic between dimensions wasn't good because it creates a tunnel of energy that makes it easier for us to cross – but also for those that we don't want to cross."

He remembered that conversation and what she said was true, but she'd just pulled that out of her head as an excuse. In a gentle, but firm tone, he said. "Maybe figure out how to communicate with her using the stylus or telepathy and leave it at that. The visits can't continue. We don't want them coming to our dimensions and you really don't want them over here. That was the whole point of creating their new home. Remember?"

She nodded. "I know. It would be great to stay in touch with her, though."

"Yes. It would." He waited a moment. "But let's not

forget her father, the group that kidnapped her or the lessons of my people. The Louers are a warring group. I'm not going to make a blanket statement and say they can't be trusted…but…"

Her knowing smile set him back. "You can't even begin to say anything like that. Paxton is a mainstay in your world. He's a pillar of the community. And he's a Louer."

"He might not know it either," Eric quickly defended his mentor. He wanted to ask him about that little bit of hidden history, but didn't want to do it at a distance. In person Eric would have a better chance of seeing the truth on his mentor's face.

He brooded on the consequences of the council finding out. Would it matter after all this time? Or could the reaction be even worse with the recent battle between the Torans and the Louers?

Was there any way to make peace with them all?

Having been raised with the shadowy specter of the Louers all his life, he hadn't noticed that threat on a conscious level, but on a subconscious level he had. His people were a simple folk. His gaze landed on Tammy. Like she was. She didn't deserve to be part of an ongoing war. Her people needed help to re-establish a new, better life in their new dimension. What was the chance he could help them do that?

Except Tammy's people were perceived as the enemy. Eric *might* want to see things workable between them. But he was pretty sure that other than Tammy, every other Louer would want to see him…dead.

Chapter 16

S TOREY WATCH THE emotions flit across Eric's face. Normally it was hard to read what was going on inside in his head. But all this talk of Louers gave her a good inkling. Finding out about Paxton's history had to be a shock.

They needed to get moving on fixing her world. His world had been fixed – mostly. The Louers had a new world; they might need help to settle it, but they might also refuse to have anything to do with them. Then there was *her* mess of a world.

She opened her closet door and stared. There had to be dozens of sketchbooks on the shelves inside. She'd never had this many in her life. Not only that, she didn't think that this Storey drew.

"Stylus, why?"

The world is trying to reassert itself – to heal from the time twist. In your case, the Storey who lives here is feeling repressed. And having found a whole new hobby, she's driven to reassert that part of her personality. Your mother and father are also having some personal issues in this world as their personalities try to reassert themselves as well. In real time, they were divorced, so being together now is not easy. They are struggling with their relationship.

Storey took a shaky breath. "I really messed up, didn't

I?"

Yes. That is one outlook.

She winced. "Thanks," she murmured. She reached into the closet and pulled out the largest of the sketchbooks. She sat on the floor beside Eric and leaned back against the bed. She flipped to through the pages. "The book is brand new."

"Does that surprise you?" Eric asked around a mouthful of food.

Storey shrugged. "I guess. I never had money for lots of sketchbooks. I'd have one, use it, then buy another one when I needed to."

"You never mention your currency or trade system here." He looked down at the beef jerky in his hand then back at her. "In fact, I know you call it money, but did you buy this food? All the times we've stocked up, did you need to leave some of this money behind?"

She stared at him in disbelief. Then laughed. And laughed. She twisted to see him better. "Now is a hell of a time to ask that question."

He flushed. He mumbled, "Yeah, I know. In my defense, we've been a little busy." Then he took another bite.

She grinned. "As it's my house, my mother's food, then no, I don't feel that we need to leave money to pay for what we've taken. The times where it wasn't my house, it would have been nice to have left money for them. But," she cocked a brow at him. "I didn't and don't have any."

His gaze widened. "Really? Why not?"

How to explain work and money. She had to think about it. She hadn't exactly seen any type of currency in his world either. Or a barter system for that matter. Maybe they didn't have the same system. "Well, I have a little, but not much." Her mother had given her money to go to the mall before this mess all started. And boy, did that seem like months ago. Then there was her almost empty bank account. "Do you have money?"

"Sure. We all do." He nodded. "We each get the same amount every month."

That stopped her. Wasn't that what the communist countries did here? Or some of them. Doctors and waitresses received the same or close to the same amount of money. Odd. And hardly fair. Then she wondered. "So you received the same amount of money as Paxton?

He nodded.

Weird. "And what about your father?"

He frowned. "I assume so."

She wouldn't. "I think you should look into that."

"Why would he have more than any of us?"

"What does the amount do for you?" She asked curiously. "Can you buy special things? Do extra things?"

He shrugged. "Somewhat. But we all have what we need. He does get different food and drink. His clothes cost more. So he probably needs more."

She had to bite her tongue. From her world she knew the extent people would go to for more of what they wanted. Greed was a powerful motivator. Maybe it was different in Eric's world, but she doubted it. Considering what his father already felt fully justified in doing to her, well, giving himself a larger portion of the pie would be nothing.

And then there was his size. He was way fatter than the others of the council that she'd seen. Maybe he had a thyroid problem or other health issue, but those hardly explained the triple chins. He ate more than he needed to and she suspected a richer quality food than the others too.

"You don't have much crime in your world, do you?"

They must have some, because they had dungeons, but she'd not been aware of any kind of personal danger from the others there. Funny, she hadn't considered it. The only Toran she'd feared at all was Eric's father.

"No. There have been a few criminals over the years, but not many."

She nodded. Maybe their monetary system worked then. She refocused on the problem at hand. She'd have time to study up on the Torans' way of life later. When her mother was back to normal.

"Stylus, what do I need to do?"

We need you to think about the last time you saw your mother. The way your world was then. It will take some time to bend time back properly and allow that dimension to return to the way it was. You need to make sure you don't stop the process once it starts. This will be our only chance to fix this. Once we start, we must finish.

She looked down at her sketchbook and realized she'd written the message. This time, Eric leaned over and read it himself. "Scary."

"Yeah. So when I start, you have to make sure that nothing interrupts me. Got it?"

"Got it." He took in a deep breath. "Maybe we should take Tammy home first then."

Storey looked outside and realized how late the day was getting to be. "I don't think we have time. My parents could be home soon."

"That isn't good." He hopped off the bed and crouched in front of her. "I'm not going to be able to keep them out of the room if they hear us."

She nodded. "I know." With a deep breath, she added, "But I'm starting to feel a sense of urgency about this." She glanced at Tammy. "I don't want to put her in danger. If you have to, leave me and take her back alone. You can hop back here and get me out."

He shook his head. "Oh no. If it's going to be that bad, then we don't do this right now."

"We have to," she said earnestly. "Look at how screwed up things are. Your world is almost normal. Tammy's is even better, although they might not think so yet, but my world is a mess. We're here and I can't help but feel the longer it stays like this, the harder it will be to change."

The Broken One spoke, shocking Storey as he once again took over her mouth, "She is correct. This must be fixed before it is too late."

"Damn." Eric glared at her, but she knew it was more at the Broken One than herself. "Fine. I don't like this, but the sooner we get it done the sooner it's over with." He looked around the room. "Maybe you should sit in the closet or something in case someone does come."

She looked at him in shock. "Why not just lock the door. I don't really want to sit in there."

"Because I presume your family could get in if they needed to. In the close—"

"They'd still find me. It's not like the closet opens to your world or anything." She thought about that. "Now that would be an interesting way to have a portal."

"Don't even think about it. Let's do this fast and go home." He glanced at Tammy, now watching them avidly. "Although, I'd rather get Tammy home first."

"Torrey." Tammy held out a piece of cracker.

Storey smiled and took it. She munched it carefully, staring at the little girl that had become so much a part of her life. "Stylus, we won't be going back in time, will we? I won't lose my memories of these people – right?"

There was no answer.

In her mind she could hear a weird humming as if the Broken One was considering the issue.

In horror she stared at Eric. He reached out and grasped her hand. "Don't even begin to think that. I was in your life before you twisted time. I'll be in your life afterwards."

She searched his eyes. On impulse, she reached up, captured his face between her hands and kissed him. Pulling back, she whispered, "Just in case."

He smiled, a tender smile that melted her heart. "In that case…" he leaned forward and kissed her. His kiss wasn't smoking hot like when he'd kissed her In-between, or even heated…but it was unbelievably tender. It brought tears to her eyes.

He brushed her hair with his hand. "Hey, none of this. It's going to be fine."

She sniffled the tears back. "Right. Stylus. Please confirm that my memories will remain intact."

"We have discussed this. We are not expecting to affect any of your memories," said the Broken One. "We cannot be sure what might happen unexpectedly."

She crooked her head. "I guess that's the best we can hope for."

With a final glance at Eric, she settled back. "Then let's get this done."

ERIC SAT BACK on the bed, and reached absently for another of the unusual beef jerky strips. He pulled the last one from the bag and it was snatched from his fingers. His gaze widened as he tracked the piece back to Tammy. She popped it into her mouth and laughed silently.

"I would so love to communicate with you, Tammy," he said. Her smile was so infectious and she chewed with such joy that he chuckled. "Minx."

She offered him the last little piece now all gummed up in her fingers. He barely managed to keep from pulling back in horror. He shook his head and pointed at her. She popped the last bite into her mouth and licked her lips. He grinned. At least she was enjoying it.

He turned back to Storey, head bent, she focused on the paper pad in her lap. Her hand was in the start up phase of her drawing process and she covered the page with large, casual strokes. He knew before long he'd barely be able to discern her hand movements as they would speed up faster than his eyes could follow.

Odd to think Paxton had possessed a stylus for over a century now, and never did any type of artwork. Thinking of Paxton, Eric realized it was a good time to let him know what they were doing. He snorted. That's all he ever seemed to do when Storey was out of commission. Ferry information. At least it made him feel useful.

He sent his mentor a message via codex. And received the answer back that Paxton already knew. The styluses had updated him. And that was a good thing. It saved time and energy to have everyone on the same page – to borrow one of Storey's turns of phrase. But, he couldn't say that he was entirely comfortable with this communication system that kept everyone informed – except him.

At one point he'd suggested to Storey that they hide away in her dimension from those of his world looking to kill him. Now he realized that would be harder than ever to do. The styluses could communicate with each other at will.

He doubted that they'd listen to Storey's request and not pass on information about their whereabouts. Especially if they considered they had a better way for events to play out.

In fact, other styluses would volunteer the information before being asked.

That meant secrecy was out. In fact, privacy was also out. How did that affect his relationship with Storey? He hadn't had much quality time with her, and he'd been looking forward to a time when it was just the two of them in a time of peace. Sure his job required him to travel often, but it wasn't the same as in her dimension. He glanced out the window. In the blue sky he saw the scars in the air made by the flying cars. Planes. He'd studied everything about Storey's world that he could. The archives were surprisingly complete. Storey had been a well of information as well.

Nothing he'd learned would convince him to go inside those metal death traps. The ones on the road were bad enough, but to think of trying to lift them into the air and let them fly like her people did…well. He shook his head. Not for him.

Something growled outside the window. He kneeled on the bed and looked out the window. "Shit," he whispered hoarsely. A vehicle was driving up the driveway to Storey's house. "No, no. Not now." He spun around and searched the room. Maybe Storey could stop – they could get the hell away? No, Storey's hand was moving over the sketchbook so fast he could barely see the flesh of her fingers.

Damn. She was in the zone. With the stylus's warnings fresh in his thoughts, Eric realized they couldn't afford to get caught here. He jumped off the bed and ran over to the door. He flicked the lock closed and turned off the light. What were the chances that the family wouldn't come to her room? That they'd stay downstairs until Storey was done and they were gone? He had no explanation for their presence…or Tammy. He also couldn't allow anything to stop Storey. This whole dimension would be shifting soon. After they did a reset – whatever that meant. But they had to get the hell out of here before the changes took effect or the changes would impact them too. That also couldn't be allowed to happen.

Then he heard people downstairs.

"Please don't come upstairs. Stay down there." He closed his eyes and waited.

And sighed with relief when there were no footsteps on the stairs. He could only hope Storey's parents would stay downstairs a little longer.

He reset his codex for Paxton's lab. If there was no other option he wanted to make sure that he got Tammy away. He could take her back to her dimension, but if her father was there waiting for him, he might not be able to come and help Storey when she needed it, and that came first.

Paxton would not appreciate seeing Tammy again. Eric closed his eyes as he leaned against the locked door. "Hurry up, Storey. Aren't you almost done by now?"

Storey didn't answer.

Head bent over, she was frozen in place while all her energy appeared to keeping her arm moving at an impossible rate. He closed his eyes, his heart pounded and his blood pulsed. *Storey, faster.*

Footsteps sounded on the stairs.

CHAPTER 17

S TOREY WAS AWARE of her surroundings. Aware of palpable waves of urgency coming off of Eric. Aware, but not able to speak with Eric, or her stylus. At least she didn't think she could. Just as the Broken One had taken her over her vocal cords at will, it now controlled her arm like she'd never experienced before. When her stylus drew through her, she was still aware on some level what was happening. In this case, it was like there was a wall between her and the understanding of her actions.

She was grateful she hadn't been put to sleep this time. Yet being awake gave her a whole new level of perspective. The Broken One had taken over so quickly, she'd barely understood it was happening at the time. She could only put it down to the fact that she'd been accustomed to her stylus for so long.

And so long only meant what…a little more than a week? She couldn't believe that was all it had been since she'd met Eric and the stylus had come into her world. In her peripheral vision she saw Eric walk over to the door. He stayed at the corner of her vision. She wished she could ask him what was wrong. But she already knew. He was worried about her. About being caught. About how long it would take.

She wished she had answers. She closed her eyes and

tried to relax. Inside, her stomach knotted. If this took much longer it would drive her nuts. And Eric. She peered in the direction of Tammy. And inside she smiled. Tammy had curled up into a ball and appeared to be sleeping.

That was good. A quiet Tammy was heaven. If she was startled awake…so not. She tried to relax further, willing the styluses to finish. She had no idea how they could do what they were doing, but she remembered sitting in the dark in her den for hours while she created the first mess that they were now trying to fix.

Please hurry, she whispered.

We are.

She groaned silently. Then stilled. What was that? Oh no. Footsteps in the hallway. They had company. She caught and held her breath.

Please don't come to my room. Please don't.

Had she remembered to lock the door? If they found the door locked, then what?

Please don't come. She chanted silently in a mantra that wouldn't quit, while her hand blurred with speed.

"Storey, are you home?"

Her eyes flew open. And stared into Eric's wide eyed panic. He mouthed silently, "What do we do?"

She couldn't move her head. Eric tapped his codex. She widened her eyes. She blinked several times. He straightened.

"Storey. Are you in there?"

They froze.

Eric tapped several keys on his codex. She held her breath waiting for the musical notes to fill the air and give their presence away. Only they didn't come.

He stepped over to Tammy and struggled to pick her up. Sleeping, she was a dead weight. He managed to straighten, shifted her in his arms, and pressed the final button to go. She watched as he stood in the middle of the smoke. She hated that he was leaving. That she was being left behind. Tears welled up inside as she watched them disappear in front of her.

He mouthed at her, *I'll be back.*

She managed a tiny nod.

As she watched the smoke disappeared.

Her bedroom door rattled as someone grabbed the door knob.

"Honey, what are you doing?" Her father's voice came from down the hallway.

Surprisingly close, Storey heard her mother say, "I wanted to look and see if she was there."

"You know she's not. She's run away. I don't know what happened, but we have to let the police handle it. Like they said they would."

Her mother's voice made her want to cry out. There was so much pain and loss threading through it. She wanted to tell her mother that it would all be okay. But she couldn't. There was no guarantee that it *would* be okay. She didn't know what would happen after this point. Would there be anything left of them? Would her mother be happy to *not* have her father again? Would she have any lingering emotions from this blip on her screen?

Storey hoped not. But she didn't know and she hated the doubts. The fear. Maybe she wasn't doing the right thing.

Was it possible that she should leave well enough alone?

AS SOON AS the black smoke blotted Storey and her frantic

drawing from his sight, Eric knew he'd done the wrong thing. Hell. His nerves bit at him.

He shouldn't have left her alone.

She was defenseless in this state. It didn't matter that she was at home. Her parents didn't know her. Not like he did. In fact, these parents didn't know anything about her. They were from another reality.

He shifted his feet wishing the black smoke to disappear. If anything happened to her before he could get back…

"Hurry up. Hurry up."

He glanced down at Tammy, who slept in a deep, relaxed manner. Thankfully. She might not be so impressed with waking up without Storey. If she opened her mouth…Eric shuddered. Tammy's secret weapon was that cry of hers. And he did not want to hear it again.

At least at home, Paxton's stylus should be able to communicate with Tammy. Enough to keep her calm so he could get away. He wanted to return for Storey. Of course that wasn't likely to go so well with Paxton. Neither was it fair on Tammy. She was a sweetheart. She should be home, safe with her family.

The mist dropped low enough Eric could see the familiar white walls of Paxton's lab. Thank you! He strode out of the portal and over to the empty table. Barely holding back a groan, he carefully placed Tammy down. His back screamed as he straightened. Tammy might be young, but she, like the rest of her people, was stocky.

"Eric," Paxton called from the far side of the room. "Is that you? Is it all done?" He rushed over then came to a screeching halt. "Oh no. No. No. No. That's not good."

"No it isn't." Eric gently stroked Tammy's hair. "But I had no options. I have to leave her with you." Not giving

Paxton a chance to argue, Eric ran back to the portal crying out, "I have to help Storey."

"No!" Paxton ran toward him, his voice squawking loudly. "Don't leave her here."

"I have to." The black mist rose as the reassuring musical notes floated out. "I have to rescue Storey. I'll get back as soon as I can."

And the black mist rose up to block out everything.

Chapter 18

"HONEY, YOU HAVE to stop haunting her room. It's not normal. You have to let it go."

"I can't let it go. I can't let *her* go. She's my daughter. She's my life."

Storey listened to the voices yelling outside her door, then a bang as something hit the other side of her bedroom door. Her mother started weeping. Not a gentle crying, but heart wrenching sobs. Storey would have bawled herself if she could. Instead she was frozen in her own body as her hand whistled across the page.

She hated the pain she'd caused her mother. In either world. How had things gone so wrong? In trying to make things right, she'd ended up making things so much worse.

"Now, come on. Let's go downstairs and get you a cup of tea. That will make you feel better."

The crying jag became muffled. Storey could only hope her father was holding her mother. Comforting her as Storey couldn't. Their voices were barely audible as their footsteps receded down the hallway. Her mother's sobs slowed the further away she went. Much to Storey's relief.

It is well, the Broken One said.

If you say so, Storey muttered restlessly. *Are you almost done?*

Yes.

She shuddered in relief. *Then what?*

We exit this dimension.

Good. Then let's go to the closest or fastest point. She thought about it for a moment. *On second thought, let's go wherever we cause the least amount of damage.*

Paxton's lab.

She closed her eyes. She couldn't remember what they'd said before. *Wasn't it supposed to be the Louers' dimension?*

Tammy is with Paxton.

Right. Tammy needed to go home. To avoid too many cross traffic scenarios, better to go to the Torans' dimension, then back over to the Louers' dimension. Of course Paxton wouldn't think much of that either. He wouldn't want them to go directly to the Louers' as that would make it easier for the Louers to travel to his dimension.

Arrrg. This was getting so confusing. Why couldn't it be easy?

She'd made life complicated by crossing over to the Louers' dimension. And meeting Eric. But that was a good thing. Not a complication. Keeping a relationship going – now that was a complication. How were they going to do that? She wasn't ready to leave her dimension and doubted Paxton would be willing to have her permanently anyway.

She stilled. Something had changed. What? She opened her gaze and studied her bedroom.

Her hand had stopped moving.

She stretched out her arm and gave it a good shake. It throbbed like crazy. Not injured, but bruised and aching as if she'd hung onto a tree branch or something for a long time before dropping to the ground. The elbow joint was especially bad.

Moving stiffly, she struggled to her feet and caught a

glimpse of the top of her bed. Food wrappers and empty boxes, cracker crumbs and napkins littered the crumpled bedding. All she did was clean up behind those two. She smiled. They felt like a family already.

A whisper of sound behind her had her spinning around. She held her hand to her head as the room twisted crazily. Why was she starting to feel faint? Weak.

Black mist filled the room. Eric.

She smiled brightly. "Yes! Perfect timing. We're done."

Eric stared at her through the blackness. But he never said a word. It was as if he couldn't see her.

She waved her arms back and forth in front of him. "Eric? What's wrong? You're scaring me."

The black mist slowed worked its way down his body. He opened his mouth and closed it again. His gaze spanned the room before zooming back to her. "Storey?" he asked hesitantly.

"Uh oh. Do I look different? Sound different? What is it?" She turned to look around her room. It looked as it had before he'd left. A mess. Normal. She, on the other hand, felt sick. Like really sick. Not the upchuck type of sick, but a woozy pass-out-kind-of-sick.

She took a step and wavered. She started to panic. *Stylus. What's wrong here?*

Silence.

Stylus. Talk. To meeeeee. She collapsed to the floor.

But she did hear Eric's voice, calling, "Storeeeey?"

"OH NO. STOREY, where are you?" Eric called out, desperation and panic filling him. He couldn't move yet for the mist, but he couldn't see her anywhere. The door was closed, but he couldn't tell if it was still locked from the inside. She should be there.

As he looked around he caught sight of something faint, like a misty outline of something, but it wasn't clear enough to identify.

"Paxton. Is Storey still in the same location?" His fingers tapped the codex frantically, fumbling to get it right as he stayed…stuck in the portal. And then he realized that's what he was. Stuck. Had he come back during the reset? Whatever that meant. Was *he* now caught between time?

Clearly something odd had happened. He hadn't even questioned the repercussions of his return jump on Storey. He'd acted out of instinct. Fear. The need to save her. He'd presumed she'd still be there.

And she was…or some part of her was.

Or was he going crazy? He was locked into his portal. Outside the black smoke, the room looked the same. And to make matters worse, he could hear someone racing up the stairs in the main house. He couldn't move. And if that wispy image was Storey, it seemed neither could she.

Paxton, he tapped. *We need help and now!*

There was no answer.

"Damn it! I heard someone in there. I heard someone calling." A woman's voice cried out in pain.

That was Storey's mother. She sounded….devastated. Like her only child had died. Which, as he looked around the room yet again, his stomach muscles contracting, Storey might have. It was one thing to end up banished in the Louers' dimension and another to be dumped into In-between, but if that ghost-like essence was Storey – something was even more wrong than before.

And all he wanted was for things to finally go right.

Was nothing ever as it seemed to be? Even his world appeared to be fake. A deceptive face on reality. Paxton a Louer, their supposed enemy. The styluses, alive and also Louers, had proven to be staunch friends and allies.

His father, a betrayer, instead of his beloved leader.

Storey wasn't even what he'd always believed. In fact, he'd been raised to be afraid of the Humans. They were destroyers, he'd been told. War mongers. Instead, she was the most caring, loving, of all the species he'd met yet. And that didn't say much about his own people.

His own father had attempted to kill her – several times in fact. So who were the war mongers?

In contrast Tammy hadn't been afraid of Storey or Eric. Yet she'd been raised in harsh conditions brought about by Eric's own people. Had she been raised to hate his people? Not according to her behavior. Maybe the adults in her world hated his people, but from what he'd seen so far, the adults were fighting between themselves to try and improve their lot in life. Having seen their home world, Eric was willing to cheer them on.

Maybe Storey was right. Could they help the Louers to have a better life? Give them the tools to build what they'd need in their own world? Would that bring peace to the three worlds? Not that Storey had mentioned bringing her world into an alliance or anything. She didn't appear to be naive about her own society. She'd even mentioned that peace wasn't likely. But that didn't mean he couldn't help fix the problems between the Louers and the Torans.

The Torans had banished the Louers after all. Maybe they could rectify that by giving them assistance right now.

Or maybe he should leave well enough alone.

And then he heard the man outside the door say, "Look,

we can check. It's not that big a deal."

The door opened.

Eric stood frozen in place.

CHAPTER 19

S TOREY STRUGGLED TO her feet and stared at Eric, finally realizing he couldn't see her. What was going on?

She was supposed to leave and come back so that the changes could take place. Sure, she'd delayed her departure, but just long enough to clean up. It's not like her stylus had said go now. Hell, she didn't even have a portal ready. In fact, she'd half assumed she'd have a portal made for her and she wouldn't even know it. She'd been doing so much that was out of her control. Why not that? But this…this being here, but not being seen…was horrible. And frightening.

What was going on?

She felt normal. At least as normal as she could after having just collapsed to the floor. She had no idea what that had been about either.

She stared at her fingers.

Talk about scary. Her hands appeared normal-shaped, but they were faint, thin. As if she had been half erased or something. As if she were only half here. Her stomach bottomed out. If there was a bottom. She wore the same clothes, but she could see through them. She had shoes on. But she saw the floor underneath them. She'd become transparent.

She spun to look at Eric. Could he see the bit of her that was left?

God, she hoped so.

"Eric?"

He spun around and she gasped. His features seemed almost blurry around the edges.

"Oh thank God. You can hear me?" she asked.

"Storey? Where are you?"

"Eric, I'm right in front of you." She stepped forward again into his line of sight. "Eric, can you hear me?"

His face crinkled up and he tilted his head toward her. As if hearing something. But not her apparently. She heard the same noises he did. To her, the sounds were faint, like coming down a long tunnel. Maybe that's how he heard her, too.

Stylus? What's happening?

Silence.

That worried her more than anything else so far. She needed to connect with the stylus. It had the means to save her.

Wait. The Broken One should be with her. She should be able to communicate with him. And if she couldn't, then she didn't understand anything because he was inside her. One with her and she could talk to herself.

She heard a sound. She spun around and watched her bedroom door crack open slightly. And then it started to fade too.

She shouldn't be here. She knew that deep inside. While whatever was happening was probably good for her world, it was not good for her. She needed to get out of this place. And so did Eric.

How?

"Broken One," she whispered. "Where are you?"

A stuttering whisper slipped through her mind, her

thoughts.

Fading, he said. *Quickly.*

"Why? What's happening?" Storey needed answers. And fast. That was the only way she'd get out of this.

The dimensional change happened more quickly than antic-ipated. This dimension was already trying to revert back to its natural state, but there were just enough changes that it couldn't. Now that we have unlocked the restraints the dimen-sion is spontaneously swinging back to the way it should be.

"Am I here?"

You are caught in the dimensional shift.

There was a neutral pause, then he said, *As am I.*

"Will we die? Or is there a way to port out of here and save us?"

A weird hum filled the air. Instead of scaring her, it reas-sured her that the stylus was there, thinking. But she wanted her stylus. She'd connected to it in a different way. She needed it.

"Stylus are you there?" She waited for a long moment, feeling tears welling up at the weird sense of loss. "Stylus," she whispered plaintively. "I need you."

A rumble slipped down her spine. But inside. She shook her head at the weirdness of it all. "Can you help me, stylus?"

Stay calm, the Broken One said. *We will ride through the shift.*

"And where will we come out at the other end?" She spun around, hating the sense of panic happening inside her. The room faded in and out. Falling and then stabilizing as if the earth itself was attempting to reassert some control. Every movement she took sent her off balance. She careened from side to side trying to remain steady in an unsteady world.

At the same time, she felt like the world was tilting. She

tried to lean into the curve, sure she'd fall over. Eric stood still in front of her. Frozen. He hadn't moved, but the floor where he stood shifted – with him. His eyes had locked on the door handle and that was it. She hadn't seen him even blink.

She ran a hand through her hair. Oh man, this was beyond nuts. And scary. She hadn't been this scared since she'd dropped into Eric's dimension so long ago.

The floor, the planet, gave a hard shake.

Earthquake?

No. The dimension reasserting itself. God, what had she done?

Her head started to swim. She shook it to clear her mind, and heard the Broken One in the background.

Let go. Let yourself fall. It will be alright.

She didn't know if she could trust him. She wanted to hear her stylus tell her that.

And there, so faint it was only an impression, a whisper slipped into her mind.

All is well. Reset is happening. Go.

She took a deep breath, recognizing her stylus. And stopped resisting.

For the second time she fell, only this time, the floor, as it trembled and shook, gave one last hard ripple and rose up to meet *her*.

WHAT WAS HAPPENING? To his amazement, the view in front of him shifted and wavered like a ripple from underground. As if someone had picked up a corner of the floor like a rug and gave it a hard shake. Even the bed rippled up and down. The few items on the table flipped up into the air, only to land exactly as the item had sat before the flip.

It couldn't be an accident the way everything came back down in precisely the same way. Was this what happened when something moved *through* the shift?

Like he presumed he had when he'd arrived at the start. If Storey had still been there at the time, he figured she'd be like the bed, and land exactly where she'd been at the start of the shift. But the styluses had said she was supposed to leave the dimension and then return.

Had she done that? Had her trip gone wrong – like so many other trips? Was the whispery version of her that stood in front of him residual energy? He closed his eyes on that thought. Please not.

He tried to move again, but his feet were cemented to the floor. He could lean and twist but he couldn't take a step. As everything else rippled around him, he appeared to be caught and held in the eye of the storm. The portal mist swirled in place around his feet. Protecting him? Or unable to complete the port because the conditions were too unstable?

Either was probably in his favor.

Then what about Storey?

Another hard ripple zapped the world. He closed his eyes and rode the wave.

How long could this last?

This ripple wasn't slowing. Fear clutched his heart. Why wasn't it stopping? The mist around his feet snugged up close. Then the tendrils wrapped around his legs as if clutching him tight. He could only think he was being held down.

Pressure built around him, his head started to pound, his chest squeezed tight. He gasped for air. His vision blurred.

He tried to focus, but every movement was like plowing through molasses.

Something was wrong. Storey? Paxton? Someone?

He couldn't breathe. His chest clamped and locked with his next breath. Black spots appeared before his eyes and his ears pounded. He felt himself falling, but the portal mist had climbed higher up his legs, as if trying to escape this hell as well.

He couldn't hold on any longer. Pain took out his senses, weakened his resolve. He needed help.

Now.

Then another mighty shove sent the world slamming up against him. A gasp escaped, taking the last of his air with it.

Storey, I'm so sorry.

And he lost consciousness.

CHAPTER 20

STOREY WOKE TO a hell of a headache. She could barely open her eyes. And wasn't sure she wanted to make the effort. What happened? Then she remembered. Her and her brilliant idea to fix the chaos she'd created messing around with things she shouldn't.

That she'd done it all with the best of intentions didn't matter. Now she had to deal with the results of this latest mess. Had her world reset? Was it back to normal? Or was she not that lucky?

She hadn't been lucky yet.

Even as she thought that, she chastised herself for ignoring all the good things that she'd done. And the people she'd met through her actions. She had to believe it was all for the best and things would work out.

Still, the teen who'd been so despondent over the loss of her boyfriend seemed a long ways away. She'd grown and then some.

Would anyone else notice? School seemed so juvenile. And so…necessary. And didn't that beat all. She'd not had any purpose to going before, except that it gave her a reason to get up and do…something. She hadn't been lost, but neither had she been found. If that made any sense. Not that anything did these days.

She'd been gone from school for so long. Everyone

thought she'd been sick to begin with. So now they'd think she'd been *really* sick. She giggled at her earth humor. Not that her black wit was helping her adjust to the current mess.

Her body ached like she'd struggled through a thorny thicket barely ahead of a bear. Her skin had taken on a scraped, raw feeling – from the inside out. She tried to take stock. With her eyes closed, she wiggled fingers, then toes. She rotated her ankles and shifted her legs. Rolling onto her back she stared up at the blue sky. Then closed her eyes again.

And had to wonder. Who's blue sky was it?

Where had she landed? She'd been inside her bedroom before the shift. And if she could move her body, did she have a real body or only that weird, ghostly, half-there-half-dead-and-gone version? To find out would mean opening her eyes again. And that hurt. Like the rest of her. Her neck was stiff. Her throat felt swollen, too large for her mouth.

Kind of a horrible feeling, actually.

She groaned. And at least heard that. So she had a voice, and her ears worked. But that didn't erase the feeling of having survived a bomb blast.

Then she remembered just what that bomb had been.

Her home. Eric. Her mother.

She sat upright, and gasped. Clutching her head, she had to wait for the world around her to stop spinning.

It slowed enough that she could straighten a little more. She dropped her hands and looked around. She was out in the country on a beautiful day. The sun was high, there wasn't a cloud in the sky.

Did that mean she was in Eric's dimension?

Only there was no sign of Eric. Damn. No sign of Tammy, or her home. Moving slowly she stood up and smiled happily. The world no longer rotated. Even her headache was dissipating.

Still, as she looked around she realized there were no paths in the meadow, no roads, no signs showing which direction she should travel. Neither did she recognize any landmarks.

Hell.

She suddenly remembered her stylus and slapped her hand to her chest where it hung around her neck. It was there. Thankfully. Then she frowned. Even that was different. The connection was different. Disconnected, yet whole for the first time, so maybe the better term was reconnected. Stronger. Some of the rawness had eased and like putting on a new set of clothes, she wiggled to settle in better.

And what was with the Broken One? Was he still with her?

Yes.

She grinned. "Hey you survived. That's great. What about you, stylus, are you in there?"

Fainter, weaker than the Broken One, the answer was audible. *Yes.*

She did a happy jig. "Good. We all made it. That's excellent."

She spun around, feeling stronger and more alive than she'd expected to feel. After what she'd been through…she could have died. But she hadn't. She was here, alive and well and still had both styluses safe and sound.

Life was good.

"So, where are we?"

A noise sounded behind her. She turned slowly to see several Louer warriors coming toward her, each holding long poles like the two warrior women she'd seen on her first visit to their dimension. The air whooshed out of her. *Damn.* She switched to speaking mentally. *Stylus, Broken One. I need a little help here. You need to tell these Louers that I'm not here to hurt anyone.*

We did.

And?

No answer.

Come on guys, they're getting closer. I could use a way out.

They know you have Tammy. They are not happy.

Storey eyed the look on the approaching Louers' faces. Stone-faced as usual. How could anyone tell if those people were happy or mad? Well the damn poles pointing at her gave her some indication.

Did you explain that Tammy leaving with us was a mistake? That I'll happily go and get her?

They don't believe you.

Just then a high pitch sound screamed through her head. She knew what was coming. *Tell Paxton. Eric. Get help.*

And the world around her went black.

She pitched forward to the ground. Out cold. Again.

"ERIC?"

His shoulder was shaken, then again harder. "Eric, wake up.

The next shake hurt. He groaned in protest. "Stop. I'm here. I'm here."

"Then sit up. I need to make sure you aren't injured."

"I'm fine." But he rolled onto his back and stared at the white ceiling tiles of Paxton's lab. And then his gaze landed on Paxton. His mentor's face flushed, then grew pale, then flushed again as waves of emotion rolled across his face. His hair, normally slicked back, was standing on end, giving him a frazzled appearance. An appearance that had become much more common these days. He let his eyes close again.

"You don't look fine," Paxton snapped. "You've been unconscious for a long time."

Eric snapped his eyes open. "How long?" He struggled to sit up. "Where's Storey?"

"I don't know. To both questions. I wasn't here when you arrived so I don't know how long you were out. And you arrived alone. I was going to ask *you* about Storey."

Eric tried to remember what had happened. There had been that weird, world-tilting scenario in Storey's room. That had been crazy. But Storey had been there. Or part of her had been. He just didn't know what part, where the rest had been, or where any of her was now.

"Can you talk to your stylus? Contact hers?"

Paxton scurried for his stylus and tablet on his workbench. Eric struggled to his feet. He was so glad to be home. But not if Storey wasn't there with him. Damn that girl. He needed her to stay out of trouble for once.

"Where's Tammy?" He looked around. Where was the little girl? Had Paxton taken her home? "Paxton, what happened to Tammy?"

Paxton spun around, horror on his face. "She should be here. She has to be."

Eric groaned. "Didn't you feed her? Talk to her? Get the stylus to talk to her?"

Paxton's eyes grew round. He became even more flustered. "I never thought to. I couldn't talk to her. She was sleeping. I just left her to sleep. In truth I'd hoped she wouldn't wake up until you returned. I didn't know what else to do with her."

"She's a child Paxton, you can't just forget about her. She's also a Louer. Do you have any idea what kind of trouble she can get into out there?" Eric was almost shouting as he stumbled forward, fear helping to power up his strength as he ran through the lab and conference room, searching under and over all the furniture. "Tammy?"

"Tammy, where are you?" He spun around to the helpless Paxton who stood in the middle of the room wringing his hands. "Ask your stylus where she is."

Paxton's face brightened and he raced back to his stylus.

Eric groaned softly. He had to remember that using the stylus wasn't intuitive for Paxton. For Storey, using her stylus had become instinctive.

"It says she's here," Paxton announced.

"Where?" Eric chomped down on his impatience. "Where is here?"

"In this room apparently." Paxton spun around, staring at the empty lab. "But she's not. Is she?"

"No. She's not."

And that wasn't good.

"What's going on, Paxton?" His voice took on a demanding tone. He hadn't intended that, but worry eclipsed everything, including manners at the moment.

"I don't know," Paxton muttered, shaking his head. "I am trying to find out."

Eric reined in his impatience. Pushing Paxton wasn't going to help. To make sure, he strode across the room and checked the main door to the lab. Locked. Even Tammy couldn't have undone this door. She had to be still here. He glanced at the portal. "Could she have activated the portal in any way?"

"No no. She couldn't." Paxton's terrified gaze zipped

from the portal to Eric and back to the portal. He shuddered and bent his head over his stylus and muttered, "Not possible."

"Well something happened to her."

Eric couldn't stand doing nothing so he searched the entire room again. "Where had she been sleeping?"

Paxton waved off in the direction of the far corner. "I moved her over there."

There was a blanket on the floor.

Eric strode closer then came to a shuddering stop.

The blanket moved – slightly. But it lay on the ground flat. He crouched down to view the surface of the blanket from a different angle. Oh no. He bowed his head. "Paxton," he whispered, "We've got a problem."

"Yes. Yes, I know," Paxton snapped. "I'm trying to get answers."

But Eric already had one answer. He could see the vague outline of some energy. He could only presume it to be Tammy. Probably caught in the same dimensional shift as Storey, Tammy was almost invisible.

So where was the rest of her?

And if that had happened to Storey, where was she?

CHAPTER 21

STOREY WOKE TO the king of all headaches. Why? Then she remembered the Louers and their damn telepathic weapon. Man, if her people could figure out how to do that…

Part of her was getting royally pissed off over getting knocked out so often. With effort, she managed to assess her latest location. She was alone and there appeared to be nothing around her. Dirt walls and, she patted the flooring, dirt floors. And a squared off ceiling. How much had the Louers managed to build in the short time they'd been here? Probably not much.

She stood and walked the room. It reminded her of the room she'd been banished to in their old dimension by Eric's father – just much smaller. With that in mind she said, "Lights on." No lights. "Door open." No grating sound to say that a door had opened. So maybe they hadn't gotten that far yet in their building. "Stylus? Some suggestions for getting out of here would be good."

She turned around and jumped back, her hand slamming to her chest. Two female Louer guards stood in front of her. Damn. They motioned her to the side. She smiled amiably and followed their instructions.

"Ah Stylus. Could you please tell them I mean no harm?"

They don't believe you.

"Is this about Tammy again? If they let me leave I promise I'll bring her back."

Yes. They believe you are responsible.

"I returned her last time," she protested. "I've never cheated them. Lied to them. Why won't they believe me?"

This isn't the group that loves Tammy. This is the group that captured Tammy and held her hostage. They have reconciled with Tammy's father, but now this has happened and they believe you are responsible. They have Tammy's body. But she is unconscious and they are being blamed. They need you to fix this.

What? Tammy's body? Only her body? Damn. When was she ever going to catch a break? "Did we do this to Tammy?"

Yes. She should have been in her dimension when the shift happened. Everyone needed to be in their own dimension. Or connected to their dimension in some way. Like Eric.

"But I was in my dimension. It didn't help me," she grumbled.

You are the only one that needed to leave your dimension.

Ah shit. Just to clarify, she asked, *So Eric is all right, but he took Tammy to Paxton instead of home, so she wasn't in the right place when this happened?*

Correct.

Storey remembered how odd Eric had looked. So faint, yet so distinct because of that weird shift. She stopped walking. He'd been caught inside the portal. "Is Eric okay?"

Yes. He was locked in the portal. He saw and felt the shift, but was safe inside the tunnel.

She released her pent up breath. "Thank heavens for that."

A pole poked her in the back – hard. She jumped back. With a hand up to say okay silently, she moved in the direction indicated, finding a doorway opening in front of her.

Going back to telepathic communication she asked the stylus to tell Paxton what had happened.

We already have. They have Tammy.

Wait. She came to a dead stop and whispered mentally, *You said Tammy was here. And unconscious.*

Yes.

How can she be unconscious here, but be with Eric and Paxton in the Toran dimension?

She was caught in the dimensional shift. Because she should have been home, part of her went there, but as she was actually in another place, part of her stayed there.

Storey stumbled. *You're saying she's been split into two!*

Her soul, her spirit, is in the Torans' dimension. Her body is here.

How are we supposed to fix that? And fast? Poor Tammy. Storey hated to hear she'd been hurt. And in such a way. Eric was right. She should have turned right around and returned her to her home after the little Louer had snuck into the transfer with them. Her father had to be going nuts right now.

Hence the guards. Damn.

Stylus, do you know how to fix this?

We need to bring Tammy to her body.

Right. That sounds so easy.

And so obviously wasn't. She was nudged from behind again. She closed her eyes briefly then forged ahead. Where were they directing her? *Stylus, talk to them. Explain to them what we need to do.*

We spoke to Tammy's father. He thinks Tammy was deliberately hurt by this group. He insists they fix this or be banished to their old world.

Could this get any worse?

Yes.

I was being sarcastic, she muttered. Then she noticed where she'd been led. In front of Tammy's father. *Uhm, Stylus? I need help. Now. Can you port us out of here? Can Eric come rescue me? Someone?*

A busy hum wafted around her, filling the air. She understood that meant conversations were going on around her. Discussing her, but not including her.

"Stop it," she said crossly out loud. "Stylus. Can't I be included here?"

She glared at the circle of stern faced Louers. Damned if she was going to take the blame for this mess, too. It hadn't been her fault that Tammy had jumped her mid shift. Sure, she should have taken her right back, but she hadn't known that this would happen. Hell, how would anyone? Up until now she hadn't known such a thing as a dimensional shift and a soul split was even possible.

They think I am you.

What! She had to stop and get her mind wrapped around that tidbit. *Because you are the one speaking?*

Yes.

Well, tell them the truth.

I tried. They don't understand.

She dropped her head into her hands. Now what did she do?

They want you to fix Tammy.

She straightened with a small gasp. *That's what I want too, but can we?*

Yes.

Her shoulders sagged with relief. *Thank you. Now…what do I need to do?*

I've contacted Paxton. Eric needs to bring Tammy home. We can't move her body to her spirit so her spirit needs to come here.

Storey struggled with that. *Does he see her? Know where she is?*

Somewhat.

That did not sound good. *Does he understand what he needs to do?*

Yes, we have relayed the message to Paxton.

Nice. And what about Tammy, does she understand?

No.

And an uncooperative Tammy, even if in spirit only, was a bad thing.

ERIC STRAIGHTENED AS he realized how serious an issue this had all of a sudden become. And how unbelievable. "Paxton, she's here, but without her body."

"That's nonsense." Paxton rushed over, his face reddening with irritation. "You've been spending too much time around Storey. Now that girl has an imagination."

"Ask your stylus. I'm right. I know I am. I saw something similar in the dimensional shift. Storey looked something like this, although a little more substantial." He twisted his head to see Tammy from another angle and she did appear slightly more solid. He shook his head. The things he'd seen and experienced lately were crazy.

"Um?"

When more wasn't forthcoming, Eric straightened and

turned to look at Paxton. "What?"

Paxton held his stylus and tablet up in front of him. "We've got a problem."

Eric's eyebrows shot straight up. "Really. I hadn't noticed."

Paxton beetled his bushy brows at him. He tapped his stylus against the hard surface in an irritating series of click. "There's more. Storey is now a captive in the Louers' dimension. Apparently Tammy's body is there and is unconscious, and they are blaming Storey."

Oh great. He closed his eyes briefly. Damn the girl could get into trouble. "Don't suppose there is any good news?"

Paxton gasped and stepped closer. "My stylus says Tammy is separated from her body." He glared at Eric as if he had known this all along and was just springing it on him now. "How can this be? Surely, it's not possible?"

Eric shrugged. "I wouldn't have thought so, but..." He motioned to the blanket where Tammy lay, "Look for yourself. The blanket moves with her as she shifts." He stepped back a bit for Paxton to get closer. "The biggest issue is what are we going to do when Tammy wakes up?"

Paxton jumped back several feet at that threat. He glanced wildly from the blanket to Eric and back again as if Tammy were going to explode. "Take her away. Get her back to where she belongs." He waved his hands at Eric, "Now. Before she wakes up."

Eric stared at him in shock. "And how do you expect me to do that."

Paxton shook his head, sending his hair flying in all directions. "I don't care. But this is big trouble. She needs to go home. Now. We can't have them trying to come here after her. You have to fix this."

Eric studied Paxton. He was right. They needed to fix this, but how? He couldn't just pick up a wispy cloud and carry it to the next dimension. Could he?

"You have to fix this." Paxton was almost shrieking at him. His eyes were panicked, his face turned red and puffy. Eric was starting to get more worried about his health than about him waking up Tammy.

Then he changed his mind.

A wail filled the room and damn near killed him. Eric slapped his hands over his ears against the horrible noise. It wasn't the same as before. It was…worse. It had a disembodied sound, almost an echo that made it amplify in layers. He'd barely heard Storey earlier in her room. Tammy appeared to be able to communicate much better. Or much worse. He shuddered as the waves of sounds scraped down his spine.

"Make her stop!" Paxton ran to the far side of the room.

"Paxton? Get the stylus to talk to her," he shouted over the noise. "Fast!"

Paxton's eyes widened. He started writing with the stylus.

Within seconds, the noise stopped.

Eric glanced back down to where Tammy had been lying.

She was gone.

CHAPTER 22

STOREY WAS LED back out of the room. Tammy's father never said a word or motioned to her in any way. The styluses had been doing the communicating. But something had changed. The same two guards were taking her somewhere – but where? *Stylus, what's going on?*

You have been given an ultimatum.

What does that mean?

You have one night's passing to return his daughter to the way she was.

The way she was? Oh great. I sure hope you know how to put a spirit and body back together again.

Great. Not. First things first, she had to get out of here, then travel to the Torans' and find Tammy's spirit to bring it back here.

Got any ideas, Stylus?

You are being taken to Tammy's room now. You will be under guard the whole time.

As she tried to assimilate what the Stylus was saying, Storey was poked – hard – in the back. She spun around. "Hey, be nice." She glared at the woman staring back at her. To Storey's artistic eye, the hard angles of the woman's wide face appeared frozen in clay for the lack of emotion in it. How could they not show anything? She didn't get it.

Storey chained her anger up tighter, knowing she needed

to stay calm to get out of this place and help Tammy. That was the concern right now. Not Storey or Tammy's heavy handed father, but Tammy herself. Somehow she needed to be made whole again.

The trip this time was through a maze of caves and tunnels. She didn't know how these people had managed to dig so much so fast. They must have some advantage that the Toran and her own people didn't know about. If they were in the same cave system that she'd seen on her previous trip, it would have given them a start, but nothing like this. The hallways seemed to go on for miles. And maybe they did.

She was led into another room. And came to a complete stop.

Tammy lay on a raised surface surrounded by several Louers. She didn't know if they were a medical team, family, or more security. Nothing in their demeanor or dress gave her any clues to their association. Why couldn't these people make it easy?

Then, they were a simple folk and probably didn't have all the trappings of her own world. Tammy would be undergoing all kinds of tests back home by now if they were in Storey's dimension. She approached cautiously, afraid she'd be stopped before reaching Tammy's side.

No one moved.

She took a deep breath, then reached out to clasp Tammy's chunky hand. She was so cold. Her hand, normally hot and active, always tugging Storey in one direction or another, or squeezing tight, lay dead in Storey's palm. So not good.

Storey leaned forward to study Tammy's face. The skin hung slack, her mouth slightly open. Air whistled gently with every breath. Definitely alive, but empty. Like no one was home.

Except Tammy's hair moved. Storey's eyes widened as she understood. Skorky lay curled into Tammy's shoulder and nestled protectively into her hair. His beady eyes watched Storey's every move.

She straightened, fighting back the urge to cry. Her hot tears refused to listen, welling up in the corners of her eyes. She stared at the wall straight ahead until she could regain control.

Stylus. What are we going to do?

Wait.

She almost snorted, barely catching back the sound at the last moment. The last thing she wanted to do was give anything away to those watching her so intently. *Wait for what?* Eric wasn't going to be able to sneak in and help her out. He'd end up captive as well. And that was not the answer.

She had to get away.

No. The dimension is still settling. Any more travelling right now could be harmful. You could end up anywhere.

Damn. I thought that problem was done.

Those were big changes. It takes a little time.

I don't have time, she bit off. *Tammy needs me.*

So does Eric. He's lost Tammy.

ERIC WALKED THE room slowly. "Tammy?" He twisted around slightly so he could see Paxton. "What does the stylus say?"

"It says she's trying to go home. She's scared." Paxton's voice rose. "And so am I."

Eric ignored the last part. "Of course, she is. When she went to sleep she was at Storey's house. She doesn't know how she got here. And if she looks weird to us, we probably look weird to her." He paused, searching the room for Tammy's misty outline. "Have you contacted Storey?"

"There is only so much I can do," Paxton snapped. "I'm trying."

"Have the stylus do it." Eric wanted to shake the older man. His way of doing things was slowing the process. The styluses could do dozens of things at one time. "Remember, they can get other styluses to help."

Paxton's gaze lit with understanding and he started scribbling furiously.

"First, someone needs to talk to Tammy. Tell her Storey is with her father and that's where we want to take her."

Eric bowed his head, struggling for calm as he waited for Paxton. He thrust his hands into his pockets. He still wanted to clench them, but it was harder to in the small space.

Then he felt it.

A slight warmth against his bare arm.

"Tammy?"

The heat of his arm deepened.

"Paxton," Eric said, "I think she is standing here beside me."

Paxton looked up over at him, looked at the space beside Eric, shuddered and returned to his tablet.

Eric wasn't sure what that meant, but figured the older man had enough trouble dealing with the current scenario without Eric questioning him on it. "Tammy, it's going to be okay."

He stared down and caught the faint shape of the little girl. She was looking up at him. Like she had so many times before. His heart wrenched. He couldn't see the expression on her face, but she had to be freaking out. "Storey is with your Father. We're trying to get you home too."

Did she understand anything? He hoped Paxton would hurry up. Surely the styluses had spoken to Tammy by now. He wished he could talk to her.

Paxton spun around. "Storey's stylus and the Broken One say you are to go to the Louers' dimension and take Tammy with you."

Eric just stared. "Really? I'm supposed to just take this energy mass to the Louers' dimension? Tammy in a form they can't see and therefore won't recognize that I'm there to deliver?"

Even Paxton looked unsure on that point. Eric sighed and turned to look down at Tammy. The heat in his arm warmed yet again, as if she understood the problem. He felt like he needed to say something to her, but up until now he had to admit it had always been Storey who'd been the one to reassure Tammy.

"It will be fine, Tammy. We've been in worse scenarios before."

He couldn't think of another one quite like this though. And hoped he never would again, but after what had happened with Dillon, he realized how much he still had to learn and experience. He was just a youngster when compared to Paxton. Yet he'd experienced so much in this short time.

And that was, to quote Storey once again, 'way cool.'

He laughed. He loved Storey's attitude. She took on life like it was the greatest of adventures. Facing her troubles instead of running away. She never backed down from a fight, either. If she were in trouble right now, she'd be looking for a way out. And waiting for him to come help her out.

So he needed to find a way to do just that.

CHAPTER 23

STOREY BENT HER head, and tried to get the stylus to help her communicate. She whispered to Tammy, "I'm so sorry, Tammy. We never meant for this to happen. We're working on a solution. Hopefully it won't be much longer."

As she finished, she realized the others were listening. None of the guards stopped her though. They'd surrounded her, but had so far stayed back and allowed her to do her thing.

Now if only she understood what her thing was. Skorky lay curled on Tammy's shoulder. Its eyes locked on Storey as if it knew she was here to help. Too bad she didn't know how.

She could write on Tammy's arm, but she couldn't create a portal on her. Not without destroying her body. She had paper in one of Eric's bags – at least she thought she did, but it's not like she'd be allowed to keep it if she brought it out for long enough to do what she needed to do. Besides, as much as escaping here would be wonderful, it wouldn't help Tammy. And that was paramount.

You don't need paper.

She straightened. The guards straightened. Oh shit. She forced her shoulders to relax and gave the guards a smile. She'd forgotten how intently she was being watched. They could knock her out at the slightest wrong move if they didn't like her actions.

She had to remember that. *Stylus, what do you mean?*

You are developing more skills. Have more abilities. A surface is helpful for some things. And necessary for bigger things. Small things – no longer.

So how do we help her then?

You use your new honor symbols.

Symbols. She was trying to follow her stylus's trail of thoughts. Honestly. But at the moment, it was a leap to think she, herself, could create portals and that was just for starters. *I don't understand. You are the one that creates. Not me.*

No, it was I – before. Now it is you…and I.

She shook her head. *Not possible. You are the one that creates. I am just the tool that holds you.*

You have earned your honor marks. They carry abilities with them.

Abilities? She didn't know if she should be excited or terrified. She had yet to question how the stylus might have earned their abilities. She had no idea how the honor marks had come about, they'd simply appeared on her skin. Now she realized that the times her stylus had said they would honor her meant they would give her honor marks.

It had been magical in the beginning, the first mark simply appearing on her after she'd been recognized for a good deed. Now she understood it was so much more than that. They worked on time, energy and even dimensional shifts.

Abilities had to be earned. And learned. Hence the Broken One's higher place in their world. He'd been there the longest, learned the most, earned his position. And had the most to offer. Saving him was important.

She was a novice.

Not as much as you think.

What can I do?

Leave.

Inside she smiled. *Now that's the right answer. What about Tammy? Can I help her get back to here where she belongs?*

Yes. But not without the Broken One, her stylus said. *He must do the transition. Like he performed Dillon's transition.*

Right. So we need Tammy here. Can I leave, go to Tammy's…soul…and then bring her back here? Without the Louers knowing?

Not as you mean.

She almost groaned. Why was nothing ever simple? *How do you mean?*

You can leave your body behind. Go in the same form that Tammy currently exists.

Oh boy. Now that was a mind bender…again. *Really?*

Yes.

And you're saying I can do that without the guards noticing? How hard a process is this?

For you now, with your marks…it is not hard.

She didn't know if she should believe the stylus or not, but had no reason to doubt it after all the other crazy things he'd helped her do. *Is this something Louers can do on their own? Without styluses?*

No.

So it wasn't normal what happened to Tammy?

No.

What about the Torans — can they do that?

No.

So why is this something I can do?

The Broken One thought it would be an ability to help you as you moved through dimensions.

She tilted her head. *The Broken One?*

You earned your first marks after rescuing the Broken One and the others. We are and always have been connected. He awarded the first honor marks.

And the second?

I did

She brightened. Really? Sweet.

She wanted to ask more. About other abilities, but time was a definite issue. *How do I go to Tammy?*

You need only detach.

Only? She'd have laughed aloud if she could have. But ever mindful of her audience, she managed to hold back. *What about my body? Should I be lying down so I don't fall? Or can I just leave from here as I am now?*

There was a faint hum in the background. She stole a look at her guards to see if they'd notice. But they appeared unaware. Unless they were causing it. She'd thought it was her stylus. Maybe she was wrong.

Use the honor marks as a guide.

That came out of nowhere. Storey stared down at her arm where the marks seemed to glow and twist in place. They were almost alive. Somehow. Maybe not alive, but there was a force in there she didn't recognize. Energy of some kind. The marks, even as she watched, looked brighter, stronger. More powerful. She was drawn into the glow. Feeling the warmth of it surround her. A tingling sensation she'd never experienced before. She didn't understand. She hadn't lifted her arm, yet they seemed closer. Heat soothed her inside and out. How odd was that?

She desperately wanted to stand up. Did she dare? What

was the worst the guards could do, but push her down again? She tossed them a defiant look and stood. Skorky's head jerked back, his gaze widening. But he never shifted away from his protective stance at Tammy's shoulder. She took a step.

And left her body behind.

She froze. *Oh God. Oh God, Oh my God.*

Stylus? Have I separated from my body?

You are correct.

Her gaze widened. *How?*

You used the honor markings as a guide.

She stared down at her arm. Her physical arm. The one still resting on the bed, holding Tammy's hand. The honor marks now seemed softer, calmer and no longer moving. She gulped. Then looked down at what passed for an arm on her body now. Wispy smoke in a lovely white, with a tinge of lavender, filled the space she'd expected to have an arm. Her body was no better. Her hair no longer brushed her ears. Her clothes had disappeared, and boy did she gulp at that one. Although technically she wasn't exactly standing there in the buff, either. It was weird. She was there, but wasn't there. There was something representing clothing, but nothing she'd ever seen before. She let her pent up breath out slowly.

Well she'd done it.

Whatever *it* was.

Now what Stylus? How do I help Tammy and get back inside my body?

Think of Tammy as you last saw her. Feel the emotions of having her at your side.

Closing her eyes, she imagined Tammy beside her. Smiling and joyous; so full of life. The last time Storey had seen her, she'd been in Eric's arms. He was carrying her away to safety. Good. She needed to be safe.

And she is safe. Look.

Storey's eyes flew open. She gasped. Oh my God. I'm in Paxton's lab. She spun around; aware she was leaving wispy tendrils as she moved. Like a princess with a long train, Storey was leaving wispy bits of her new material – energy or clouds – wafting out behind her as she spun. *This is amazing. I so don't understand. But it is definitely cool.*

You can travel by thought in this form.

Thought? As in I don't need you, stylus?

She clasped her hand to her chest, afraid she'd lost the stylus, and realized she not only had no stylus, she had no chest! Her breath came out in harsh gasps as she fought to control the panic. This couldn't be, could it?

Yes. Our souls are connected to our bodies, but the physical body is not a prison. You can move freely in and out. We in the stylus no longer have bodies. They do not keep long term. But our souls are forever.

Forever. She repeated the word, really liking the concept. And this whole state of being, for all it was scary and fragile feeling, was also incredibly exhilarating and…liberating. *If only all people could realize they were more than an organic body.*

They can, but few would want the experience.

Are you kidding? This is awesome.

For many, the fear would be overwhelming.

True.

She was so caught up in the sensation and conversation it took a moment for her to hear the other voices. Eric. And Paxton. She laughed, a sound of pure pleasure pealing across the room.

Eric stopped talking, an arrested look on his face.

"Did you hear that?" he asked Paxton.

"Hear what?"

Storey grinned. Good for Eric. He was always so sensitive to her moods and presence. Maybe he couldn't see her in this form, but he was aware of something different. And then she gasped again. Tammy stood beside Eric, her hand nestled in his much bigger one. And she was in the same form as Storey, but in a slightly different color. Tammy appeared as a light blue to white energy swirling in place at Eric's side.

Did he know? Considering he was holding her hand, he must.

"Tammy!" Storey cried out.

The energy beside Eric turned, then shot toward Storey like a bullet fired from a gun. The blue energy surged around Storey, over her and then finally through her.

She'd have gasped in shocked delight if she could have, but the sensation of being one with another soul overwhelmed her into silence. She'd have shed tears if she'd had them; instead it felt like her heart was being squeezed small and so tight. Only it was beating hard and strong, because Tammy was inside, helping her.

"Oh Tammy. I was so afraid for you," she whispered.

"Torrey." Tammy's faint pudgy hand reached up to pat Storey's cheek. "I'm happy you are here."

They could talk like this. Without the trappings and physical limitations that defined their other reality, the two of them could communicate like they'd always wanted to. She wrapped her arms around the little girl and held her tight.

"Paxton. Something just happened," Eric said.

Paxton spun on Eric. "Now what? I can only work on one thing at a time."

"Well for one, Tammy, who'd been holding my hand, isn't any longer. And I think someone else is here now?"

Storey watched at Paxton spun around searching the brightly lit room. "There is no one here."

Yes, there is. Hi Paxton.

He didn't hear her. Holding Tammy close, Storey walked over to Paxton's monitor and hit the keys she needed with a little bump of her non-existent fingers. *Hi, Paxton,* she typed. *I'm here in the same form as Tammy. We're spirits. Storey.*

Both men raced over to the typing keypad.

Paxton grabbed his chest and stared at the place in front of his key panel. "That's not possible.

Eric whispered, "I sure as hell hope it is. Storey," He took a deep breath. "Please tell me you're not dead."

ERIC STUDIED THE space in front of Paxton's desk. There was a shimmer to the air, a motion to it that he didn't understand. And hadn't seen before. He asked, "Is that possible?"

The keys depressed even as Eric watched. Storey typed in the words, *Yes. I am alive. I left my body in the Louers' dimension so I could help Tammy return.*

Eric froze at the part where she'd left her body. What? He wanted to repeat Paxton's horrified rejection about that not being possible. He took a deep breath and let it out shakily. "Storey, how do you propose to take Tammy back?"

The keys tapped faster this time. The words appearing as if by magic. *Easy. The same way I came here. Tammy can travel by holding on to me.*

His mind refused to see how this was possible.

Just then the door to Paxton's lab opened up and his father strode in, two Toran guards trailing behind. "Paxton, I demand a hearing." He glared at his son. "These charges against me are preposterous. I have done nothing wrong."

Eric struggled to shift from one subject to the next. And adjust to his father's presence. He opened his mouth to say something, when his father rounded on him.

"And you, letting your father be treated this way. How dare you?" The pompous man strode across the room as if he still had the right.

Eric's felt his eyebrows shoot straight up. His father was actually accusing Eric of not standing up for him? Unbelievable. He glanced at Paxton, who appeared to have had one shock too many.

"Why are you not in your chambers under guard?" Paxton's fury was slowly rising as a tidal wave of red filled his face.

The Councilman sniffed. "Why should I be? My people are loyal to me. And not that upstart otherworlder. How dare she accuse me of such things?" He walked over to the workbench, putting his back to the others.

Eric blinked. Was he really that dense? Still, he felt himself looking to Paxton for guidance. Except, Paxton looked like he was about to yell at his father. Eric almost wanted to warn him. He glanced back and his eyes widened in horror. His father's gaze was locked on the monitor. And a fat smile had slipped out. It disappeared as Eric stepped forward and wiped the screen clean with the press of one button.

But somehow, he knew the damage had been done. He didn't need to see his father's beady eyes to know he had seen and processed Storey's explanation. And was even now looking for ways to use it.

"However, I will return to my quarters now. To make sure all is how I left it." He spun on his heels and headed for the door, leaving as abruptly as he'd arrived.

"Paxton, we have to stop him. He saw the monitor. He's going after Storey."

"How? He can't." Paxton ran over to the keyboard.

"He did already. Look at all the trouble he caused with the Louers last time. If he can get the message to them that Storey has left her body, well…" Eric didn't want to finish that thought. The stricken look on Paxton's face said it all. "Why was he walking around as free as you or I? And how is it he is free to go to his quarters? He should be going to the dungeons."

"He was taken for medical testing first. To make sure there was nothing physically wrong that could account for the change in his behavior."

"And now what, he's allowed to walk around – free?" Eric couldn't believe it. An anger like he'd never felt before surged through his veins. His fists clenched. Then opened. Then clenched again.

"No. No. He's not." Paxton ran to his control panel and immediately brought up the guard room. While Eric watched, he ordered guards to watch the Councilman's room. He was not to be allowed to leave without Paxton's permission. Paxton then warned that a full inquiry was in progress as to why his orders to place the Councilman in the dungeon after his medical hadn't been carried out in the first place.

"Do you think that will do anything? Or have we got a dissident force happening within our own people? People as loyal to him as he claims?"

"It's possible. He's ruled here for a long time," Paxton

muttered. "There won't be when they find out what he's done."

"Then we need to tell every one of them the truth of his actions. Because I don't trust him even under guard." Eric spun around to look for Storey. He couldn't see her faint energy. He hoped she'd gone back to where she belonged. But just in case, "Storey, we'll stop him. Honest."

There was no answering tap on the keyboard. No answering movement from anywhere around him.

Paxton stared wide eyed. "What about Tammy? Is she here? We can't have her running around loose. Please tell me they are still together. Tammy might have run away after your father's appearance."

Eric would have liked to run away too. He called out, "Storey? Are you still here? Do you have Tammy with you?"

"Storey? Please talk on the monitor if you are here."

Paxton and Eric stared at the keypad. There was no movement. No words appearing anywhere.

"Damn," he whispered. "I think Storey is gone." He could only hope she was okay. Had she been yanked back to her body? Gone back willingly with Tammy at her side?

Or was she still here – somewhere?

CHAPTER 24

STOREY WATCHED ERIC'S father approach. That man gave her the creeps. He was so…so…arrogant, so sure of his power. She hated that about him. And she couldn't believe he was still walking around. Why? How? Hadn't Eric said something about his father being taken care of?

Surely Paxton had followed through?

Surely?

She watched his gaze land on the monitor and realized the moment he understood the message she'd written. And the danger of his understanding.

But it was too late. The energy around her swirled as Tammy snuggled up closer. "It's okay Tammy. He can't hurt us." At least she hoped not. She no longer felt so confident that he'd be punished for his actions. She narrowed her gaze and watched as he bolted to the door. Had he taken something off the bench? Maybe not, but he was up to something. Suspicions raised, she trailed behind him as he walked to the door. Tammy stuck close by.

Storey looked down at her. Should they follow the Councilman? He was one scary dude, even if he was more of a fat merchant to look at him. She couldn't trust him, and she didn't dare let him get up to his old plans again. She had to find out what he had planned.

She knew it couldn't be good. Not for her. Or Tammy,

and she highly doubted Eric would come out on top. In fact, if the Councilman found out about Paxton being a Louer…well, he'd twist all this mess up and make it look like Paxton was to blame.

Get himself reinstated at the same time. Next week it would all have been forgotten. The scandal written into the archives for future students to study.

And that couldn't happen. She slipped out the door before it closed. She could probably think herself to the other side, but this way was natural. Tammy refused to stay behind.

Please, Tammy, stay with Eric.

Tammy's face grew mutinous and her shoulders squared. Not that she had much for shoulders. Still, she could understand Tammy not wanting to be separated from her again. Storey didn't want to lose track of Tammy either. And in their current forms, that was all too possible.

Okay, you can come. Just stay close and stay quiet.

With Tammy's nod, Storey picked up speed and raced behind the Councilman.

He swept into his chambers, the guards taking up their position outside the entrance, and headed directly to the big communication center on the far wall. With a furtive glance around he started clicking on the keypad in front of him. Within moments, a picture formed on the monitor above.

She heard Tammy's gasp before the identity of the person on the screen filtered in.

It was Tammy's father. How did they have the technology for this? As much as it surprised her, it also delighted her. They'd do just fine in their new home.

Oh Shit. Tammy tried to pull away from Storey's hand, but Storey held on. *It's not your father here in this room,*

Tammy. He's still in his home, your home. That's just an image for communication.

Tammy shook her head. She opened her mouth, and Storey cringed waiting for that horrible sound to come loose. But it didn't happen. Tammy had stopped, an arrested look on her face.

Who are you talking to, Tammy?

She blinked then pointed at the monitor.

Storey glanced at the monitor then back again. *You can talk to your father through the dimension?* Not that Tammy understood the dimension stuff. She rephrased the question, *Tammy, can you talk to your father from here?*

Tammy nodded.

Can you tell him that you are safe?

Tammy nodded again.

Good. Do that. Tell him that you are coming home. And can you also tell him… Storey stopped. Did she dare have Tammy warn her father about the Councilman? Did she have any choice?

Tammy, can you warn your father about this bad man?

Tammy's face turned fearful. She shuddered. The faint ripples of blue ripple outward like a stone thrown into a pond. *I know. I don't like him either. But he's trying to hurt me. And you.*

Tammy's eyes widened. She reached up to pat Storey's cheek. *Torrey.*

Storey leaned into the delicate touch, and smiled. *Yes.*

He is coming.

Storey froze. *Who is coming, Tammy?*

The little girl pointed to her father on the monitor.

Storey gasped, her own gaze tracking the Louer that dominated the screen. *Does he know the form you are in?*

Tammy shook her head. "*No.*"

How is he going to come here? That was so not good. He wasn't likely to come alone either. Damn. Storey glanced over at the Councilman, now pacing in front of the monitor and talking in a language she didn't understand. Apparently Tammy's father did, though. His face was getting redder and redder. Whatever the conversation, it wasn't to his liking.

Stylus, can you make it so that this conversation is recorded and a record is sent to the other councilmen and Paxton? Can you translate the conversation as well?

Yes. It is simple.

Then do it. If there are speakers to send this conversation live to all the councilmen, guards, whoever you can reach – do that as well. Broken One, do you agree? Can you do more?

His voice murmured in her mind. *Done. And more. We've taken the message to the people.*

Good. At least whatever the Councilman was up to would be recorded. Someone somewhere would stop him, surely. In the meantime, they were about to have the Louers arrive. And that wasn't good for anyone.

Tammy, tell your father not to come, we're coming home right now.

Tammy's gaze widened. She spun around as if looking for Eric and his portal. *No honey, I can take you home. Jump into my arms.*

Tammy grinned and immediately did just that.

Storey laughed. *Now. Tell your father.* Storey waited a few minutes. *Did you do it?*

Tammy nodded. *Good, then hold on and I'll take you home.*

With her arms wrapped tightly around Storey, Tammy laid her head against her shoulder. Their energy snuggled together. Good.

Stylus, please tell Eric what we are doing.

I have told Paxton.

Good enough. Eric might need to come and rescue me.

She took a deep breath and thought about her body, the beautiful pattern on her arm. She could see the glow on her arm, the warmth of the pattern. Such a weird feeling. But the warmth wasn't painful. In fact, it was invigorating.

Storey leaned her head back and smiled.

And found herself sitting beside Tammy's bed.

Back in her body.

"DAMN IT PAXTON, how does he manage to live so charmed? He should not be walking around free like that." Eric hated the thought. His father still had some supporters obviously.

It was as if Paxton aged before him. He wilted, his shoulders slumping. "I don't know. I don't understand." But he wouldn't look Eric in the eye.

Eric knew he wouldn't like what was to come. "Paxton, you need to tell me the truth, did you let him go?"

"He's not free," Paxton blustered. "But the other council members didn't believe everything I had to say. They want to give him a fair chance to explain." He looked around, a little lost, and added, "I was working on trying to bring Dillon back and didn't attend the last meeting. That's when they loosened the restrictions on him."

Dillon? Eric had forgotten about him. Eric stared at Paxton, seeing for the first time how much Paxton had devoted to helping his people. How much he'd lost personally in his lifetime. Had he ever married? Had children? Eric knew relatively little about his mentor and friend's family history. What he did know was that something was bothering him right now.

He suspected it had to do with Dillon.

He took several steps closer, asking in a quiet voice, "Is there something you want to say to me, Paxton?"

The older man's shoulders shifted as if to straighten, then finding the effort too much, collapsed again. Eric sighed. "And does it have to do with the fact that you are a Louer?"

Paxton gasped, he spun around so fast that Eric was afraid he'd fall over. His eyes took on a glassy look and the color, never much in his face to begin with, drained right away. Concerned, Eric led him to the stool in front of the workbench and pushed him gently into it. "Paxton?"

Paxton clasped his hands to his chest, gasping for air. His skin color faded to gray.

"Oh no. Paxton, hang on. I'm getting you help."

"No, I'm fine." He gasped, "Just give me a moment."

Eric wasn't too sure. Damn. He spun around looking for help. Where was Storey? She was so level headed, he could always count on her to give him a hand. But he knew she wasn't around. He knew because it felt like a part of him was missing. He'd never heard of anyone else having that feeling. He'd never thought something like this was even possible.

And that just made it all the more special.

"Paxton? Are you feeling better?" Eric bent over his friend, hating that he had to get answers from him and stress him out to this extent. But he suspected that it was Paxton's secret that had made him the exemplary mentor and council head that he was. And a potential victim to anything the Councilman wanted. If he knew about Dillon, which was possible given that he had access to his quarters and therefore to the database, he'd have been automatically updated on Dillon's arrival. Whether he knew about Dillon being a Louer or not was another thing…Paxton's life would be ruined if he did.

"Our grandparents had heard rumors about the banishment of the Louers. They were young, too young to get married and too young to be independent…but my grandmother got pregnant. They were owned by your father's family. They couldn't get free. His sires have all been the same."

"When the Louers were banished, my family hid away in the mountains. Trying to live their life alone. But the life was hard. My grandparents kept the secret, and my parents after them. I never knew I was different. Dillon was the younger by several years. My mother perished soon after his birth. My father was a simple man, he tried hard, but couldn't do much without her. He took a chance and moved into town and tried to make a go of it. He told me the whole story and swore me to secrecy. Warned me what could happen if anyone found out. In truth I kind of forgot about it. I was a Toran in every way. And besides, by then, everyone had forgotten about the Louers. My father worked hard and kept a low profile.

But your grandfather knew. He didn't do anything publicly, but one night my father disappeared. Dillon and I were still young. The neighbors took us in. And I never forgot again that what I was had to be hidden. That I couldn't be me. That my family was so bad we had to be banished – or worse."

The look in Paxton's eyes broke Eric's heart. How long did it take for history to be forgotten? One generation or two? Three maybe.

"Why did the Louers get banished?"

"My father once told me that at that time, many of the Toran people were dying. No one knew why. Because my people weren't dying, the Torans blamed them. When my people had no answers to the illness, things went from bad to worse. The Louers were treated horribly. This went on for years, and once everyone had gotten used to the bad behavior, it continued well past the point when the Torans were healthy again. But the damage had been done and the behavior continued. The Louers tried to gather together to fight the problem. They were serfs and not slaves. But the distinction became lost over time as their roles slid further into slave and master.

"When the Louers rose up and started fighting back, the Torans banished my people." The lost look in his eyes made Eric think he was looking back through time. "All those years, I did nothing to help my people and did everything to help your people. I'd hoped there'd be a way to find Dillon, but knew I had no means to help him as a Louer. But as a Toran, so much more was possible." He gave a broken cry. "He was all I had… I tried so hard, but couldn't help him."

He stared glassy eyed at Eric. "Then Storey found Dillon."

And Eric understood. "And you realized that in helping your brother, you were risking your own secret coming to light. Now that Dillon is safe inside a stylus, you are afraid for yourself."

"No," Paxton whispered shaking his head, "I don't care what happens to me anymore. I'm old. My time is done. I stayed around to find an answer for Dillon, now that I've done that, I'm happy to die. But I'd like to die here. Not be banished to that cold dark place. Look what they've done to my people. Look how they've changed as each generation had to deal with the hardships they've endured."

"They can't banish you, Paxton. Look at all you've done for my – our – people."

"They won't care when I'm gone." He looked up. "In fact, they are liable to look at you sideways too. Wonder if you can be trusted."

Eric laughed at that. "No, if they look at me that way, it will be due to my father's actions, not yours."

As if he'd heard his name spoken, the Councilman's voiced filled the air and his face appeared in each monitor in the room. It was kind of eerie.

"No. You must finish this. Our bargain still stands. You get rid of the girl and then I'll give you the means to travel to my dimension."

An odd-sounding voice answered, and a strong male's face filled the screen. "My daughter says otherwise."

A Louer male. It took a moment for Eric to understand. His heart slammed against his ribs. Tammy's father. The Councilman, Eric's father, was negotiating with the Louers against his own people.

"Your daughter?" blustered the councilman, "What does she have to do with this?"

"She says you tried to get rid of the girl already and now you are no longer in power. That you can't promise any-thing."

The councilman's face reddened. "That's not true. I have a secret up my sleeve. It will change the game entirely. I have information on the chief person who is against me. He will rue the day he went against me."

The Louer elder's face twisted. It was almost as if he

were listening to something – to someone – else. His face cleared. "Ah. You are talking about your great scientist, Paxton."

Paxton gasped. His eyes widened. Eric didn't know how to help him. He could only hope his father would never see power again after this. To have actually guaranteed that he could give the Louers travel back to his dimension – that was beyond anything. The council would be screaming over this. Even as that thought registered, the key pad on Paxton's desk lit up as multiple messages clogged up their communication system.

"Yes, yes, you see, he is not a Toran. He is a Louer. Like you."

Paxton, standing in shock beside Eric, bowed his head in shame.

CHAPTER 25

S TOREY RAISED HER head and took a deep breath. *Tammy, time to wake up.*

Tammy shifted on the bed. Immediately the others in the room jumped forward. They surrounded the little girl, watching intently as she started to wake up. Skorky stayed put at her shoulder, but he lifted a tiny paw to bat Tammy's cheek.

Then Tammy's eyes opened. She stared at the Louers gathered around as a hum filled the air. Storey understood they were all conversing. She could probably tune in, but that damn hum hurt.

Use the honor mark.

Storey frowned. *The same one?*

No the newest one.

She reached to touch the new honor marks on her shoulders, instinctively tracing the flowing lines. Immediately the hum muted and words of a bubbling conversation filtered into her mind. The noise was too loud. She continued to trace, finding that as she went lower down her arm, the volume muted. As she traced higher, the sound rose.

She laughed. *It's a communication device.*

It's communication energy, the stylus corrected. Now you can speak with Tammy normally.

Is Tammy going to be okay now?

Yes.

"Torrey!"

Storey smiled down at the little girl. "Hello, Tammy."

Tammy smiled, a look that lit up the room and caused all the other Louers to murmur in shock.

"I guess they don't do much smiling, do they?"

Tammy shook her head. "No. But I will teach them. You showed me. I'll show them." She practically beamed. She sat up and threw herself at Storey. Skorky jumped onto Tammy's back and scurried across to Storey's shoulder, where it chattered happily.

Wrapping her arms tight around the little girl, Storey said, "At least now we can talk to each other. Let's hope we still can after I go home."

"Torrey leaving?"

Storey nodded. "I hope so. I need to go back to see my mother."

At that Tammy held out her hand to one of the Louers at her side. "You can share my mother."

The other Louer stared down at Tammy in obvious alarm.

Storey laughed. "That's okay. I have my own mother. Thank you for the offer though."

Tammy smiled. "But you don't have a father, right? So you can share mine."

The little girl's generous spirit was heartwarming, but there was no way that her stone-faced father would be interested in adopting Storey. And the feeling was mutual. Storey wanted minimal contact with Tammy's family. Still, they had a few issues to be resolved.

The Louers at her side poked her suddenly. Storey sat back and glared at them. "You could just ask me to stand up you know."

They backed up in shock. Tammy giggled. "They didn't know that you could speak"

She looked at Tammy. "But I spoke with you?"

"I didn't let them hear the conversation."

Oh boy. She had a lot to learn. Storey said, "I couldn't speak to them before, but now apparently I can." She motioned to the shimmering marks on her shoulder.

Tammy gasped, she pointed to the marks. Skorky jumped to Tammy's arms. "Mutre, look."

Mutre, which Storey could only surmise meant mother, bent closer. Something shifted in her eyes, but so quickly Tammy didn't recognize the emotions. Shock maybe. Understanding. Definitely something along that line. It wasn't like Storey could speak Louer herself, more along the line of bad translation. Most of the message came through, but some of the finer nuances were lost.

"Tammy, what's going on?"

"Potre wants to speak to you. And to make sure I'm okay." She scrambled off the platform and grabbed Storey's hand. "Come on."

She tugged Storey to her feet and ran down the hall, holding on tight to Skorky. "It will be fine. I promise."

That the little girl was mimicking Storey's own words probably meant she didn't understand their real meaning. Tammy's father wasn't going to like anything about Storey. But she hoped with Tammy's help, they could convince him to let her go. She needed to go back to her own family soon. And somewhere along the line she had to transfer the Broken One to his new home.

And how she was going to do that was still a mystery.

It will happen in time.

Says you, she muttered mentally. *Just help me get out of this mess, first.*

As they walked into the large cave she had to wonder again if the Torans had technology that could help the Louers out as they built their new world. Then again, the Louers obviously had skills that were far more advanced than they'd initially thought. They'd dug this vast network of caves and had the technology to communicate with the Councilman in another dimension. Although he might have had a hand in that.

The damn place bulged with Louers. Oh crap. She really didn't like the look of the room full of strangers, and not friendly ones, either. All those unsmiling faces staring at her gave her a bad case of the willies. Besides, they could knock her out in an instant. She hadn't forgotten the last time.

At that memory her feet slowed, but Tammy would have none of it. Tammy was much heavier than Storey and she giggled as she pulled Storey forward. Before she knew it, she'd reached the front of the cave to face the Louer leader.

"You are Storey?" he asked, the sound reverberating loudly outside and inside her head. For such a huge man, his voice was calm, not aggressive. Still this form of communication was beyond weird. As if they were speaking aloud, but not quite. This was almost a group conversation.

She barely held back her gasp of shock, but managed to say, "Yes."

Tammy bounced between her father and Storey. Her joy at having them both there on a relatively friendly basis was more than evident. Storey took that to mean she wasn't about to be killed.

"Why are you here?"

Her gaze widened. "To help Tammy." Then she realized

they'd never actually learned what Tammy's real name was. She quickly added, "To help your daughter."

Potre gazed at Tammy, but there was no easing of the stony look on his face.

"And the Toran with you?"

"Eric?" She frowned. "He's not with me. He's in his dimension."

"Is he? And his father."

She scoffed. "That man should be locked up."

"You are not here as his messenger?"

She reared back. "I am nothing to him. He wants to kill me."

"So I understand."

She frowned. "He wants you to take care of that." She stiffened, remembering the conversation she'd overheard in the Councilman's room. "I suppose he's willing to make a deal to get that job done."

The Louer leader nodded.

"And?" she asked in a cool voice, "What is your decision?"

He tilted his head and she thought she saw something flash in his eyes. She didn't understand, but a weird hum filled the air. Dread filled her stomach; was she about to be knocked out? Quickly, she said to Tammy, "Tammy, stop your father."

"Why?" Tammy bounced in front of her, the short tubby body surprisingly agile. Skorky raced from one shoulder to the other and back again.

"I don't want to be knocked out again." Storey said in a dry voice.

"He won't." She giggled. "It won't work anymore on you now. He already tried."

"He did?"

"Yes." Tammy laughed and danced through the room. None of the other Louers noticed or paid any attention to her. Storey didn't understand the lack of interest. "Tammy, why are there no other children?"

"There are. But not many."

As the adults were looking at her. Storey continued to ask Tammy, "Do you know why there aren't many?"

"No." Tammy danced a little jig that made Storey grin. The humor was out of place, given the silent room and situation, but hard to resist. Tammy had always been a joy.

Crossover influence. She had to stop herself and think about that. She'd definitely been influenced by Tammy. Look where she was. There's no way she'd have come to rescue the little girl – time and time again – if she hadn't been. She'd also been hoping to find a way to improve relations between the Louers and the Torans. They were one and the same, inside.

And maybe so were her people, but they were a long ways away from being ready to have a relationship with other dimensions. She couldn't even imagine trying to explain such a concept to her government. Add in all the other governments of all the other countries...and things would get very icky.

"Storey."

She straightened to face the Louers' leader. He motioned to her to move forward down a corridor. She stepped forward before the guards could prod her.

Tammy grabbed her hand, and tugged her closer. Storey grinned. It was stupid to feel so happy and carefree with her fate yet to be decided, but she'd been through so much. Done so much. How could she not want to enjoy the moment? Knowing her time with this cherub was coming to an end, Storey couldn't help, but open her arms. Tammy launched herself into them. Storey stumbled. She'd forgotten how heavy Tammy was when in her body. She gave her a big hug, the two of them laughing. Finally she put her down and the two ran forward. They ended up in another cave, darker and much smaller than the previous once. On the wall was a large monitor. Filled with the Councilman's face.

For a moment Storey was sidetracked by the apparent lack of power here and the appearance of a big, functioning monitor. Maybe her people could learn more than she thought from the Louers. From the rest of the furnishings in the room, she assumed the Louers had made good use of the doorways she'd made leading back to their old world.

The voices brought her back to her surroundings.

And her lip curled.

"Why did you walk away?" the Councilman growled. "I gave you important information. You can use it to get more of what you want."

"And I wanted to check the information." Tammy's father motioned Storey closer.

"What is she doing there?" The Councilman gasped in horror. "Kill her. She's right there. Do it. Now." His voice rose to a shout as temper and outrage rippled across his face. His color went dark and he appeared to be on the edge of an apoplectic fit.

Storey laughed. "Still trying to get someone else to do your dirty work. Does the Louer leader know that you were cheating him?"

The man at her side straightened. She kept her mocking gaze on Eric's father. "That you promised to give them technology you don't have the power to give?" She snorted.

"And of course you haven't told the Council members or Paxton either, of your deal. And what about Eric?"

"Don't you even mention my son's name. You've ruined him." This time the Councilman appeared to be hopping from one foot to the other. His rotund face twisted and reddened with temper. "Kill her."

Storey tried to not to look at Tammy's father's face. She didn't want to know if he was of the same mind as the Councilman. But eventually she had no choice. Shit. She turned to face Tammy's father. "You know…Potre….Paxton *is* a Louer. But he is also a very revered Toran scholar. And he is capable of helping you." As an afterthought, she added, "If he wanted to, that is."

There was a silent murmur behind her. "As for Eric, yes, it's true he is the Councilman's son. But Eric is not like his father. He is what his father could have been. And never will be."

She didn't know if they could understand that message. She didn't speak Louer properly.

But the stylus did. *Stylus, can you tell them? Can you explain?*

We have.

And?

He isn't sure. He doesn't trust us.

Wait…does he have any relatives who are related to any of the souls in the styluses we have? Are there any Louers today that remember styluses?

The stylus bubbled with the concept. Noise filled the back of her mind. She waited, watching the Councilman and the Louer leader glare at each other. How could she convince Potre? "Tammy, have you told your father about all the adventures we had?"

"Yes!" Tammy shouted at her. "He asked lots of questions."

"Good. Do you understand that Eric's father is asking your father to kill me?"

Tammy gasped. She cried out and her arms wrapped around Storey and squeezed her tight. "Did your father say anything about it?"

Tammy shook her head.

"Has he said anything about the new dimension, problems with the Torans? Anything at all."

This time, Tammy nodded.

"Yes? What part?" Storey bent to look into Tammy's face.

"He asked about how we went from one place to the other. The types of guards you have. Eric's guards."

Storey groaned. All Tammy had seen was her house and Paxton's lab. His father must think the two dimensions were playgrounds. Neither had visible guards and both would appear developed, but empty. Sigh.

She wondered what he had planned. And why?

The Councilman's face swelled in temper as he ranted and raved about the damn people betraying him, about their lack of appreciation and how he was going to get his own back when the traitor Paxton was shown for the liar and fraud he was.

The longer Storey listened to his rants the madder she got. Finally she'd had enough. She stepped back up in front of the monitor. "That Paxton is a Louer doesn't surprise me. And of course he had to hide his identity. When your people became sick and started dying, you blamed the Louers. Your people enslaved them. Turned them into something they weren't supposed to be. When they protested and started to fight back, you banished them. How difficult it must have been then, when so much of your knowledge went with them. The knowledge in the styluses. The styluses couldn't be renewed because that technology was lost. Because it was Louer technology. Paxton's technology created in the Toran dimension."

She gave a hard laugh. "You are such an egotistical bastard. You deserve to spend your lifetime in servitude. In service to others so you can understand an honest day's work. To teach you to give, not just take. Wait until your people find out how you let the Louers back to your world out of revenge. That you were willing to give up their safety out of spite. You never counseled your people. You have been a ruler without compassion. A monarch over serfs. Do your people understand that it was you and the leaders before you who banished the Louers, and turned your own people into their replacements? Instead of all Torans being above the Louers you made yourself above the Torans."

The last words ran through her like lightening, giving her the understanding of their truth. "How many people have you hurt by your greed? Or have you been just a rotund clown at the head of the table, while the worker bees carried on without knowing what you were really like? You couldn't even spend time with your son, could you? Be a part of raising him? You left it to Paxton."

She laughed. "So maybe he was the lucky one after all."

The stylus spoke quietly. *The Broken One remembers the time of the banishment.*

Storey nodded, sorry for the pain the Broken One had been through. "Do you realize that there are still souls that remember all this? Everything that happened when the Louers were banished?"

The Councilman spluttered. "Not possible."

"Yes, it is possible. It's a fact. The styluses carry Louer souls." She shook her head. "I rescued several that had been damaged, forgotten. Lost through time. The Broken One is alive and well. I don't remember his original name…but he is here."

Her stylus spoke. *His name was Barrat.*

Storey repeated the name aloud, "Barrat – the Broken One was once called Barrat."

A shocked hum rose around her. Excited murmurs filled the air. Storey didn't understand what they were saying and she couldn't take the time to work it out as she was trying to keep two conversations together at the same time. The Councilman shrugged. "So. He is nothing to me."

"Maybe, but from the reaction I'm getting here, he means something to the Louers."

Potre leaned forward, his commanding voice breaking through the rest of the noise in her head. And spoke to her directly – for the first time. "What do you know of Barrat?"

She turned to look at him. "Everything. I carry his soul."

ERIC AND PAXTON stood shoulder to shoulder as they watched the byplay between the Councilman and Storey with Tammy's father popping on screen every once in a while. Eric was horrified at his father's machinations.

"Barrat? Barrat," murmured Paxton. "Why do I know that name?" He grabbed up his stylus and asked him for information on Barrat. The stylus started writing, filling the tablet in no time. "Barrat was the leader of the Louers. Enslaved by the Torans and sent to join the stylus when he became too old and broken to work. His knowledge was important, but his physical presence too dangerous." Paxton looked at Eric.

"How is it that Storey is carrying him? She can't have bonded to two styluses."

Eric winced. "I guess you weren't told all the details, huh?" At Paxton's wide eyed stare, Eric nodded. "You know Storey, she can't leave anyone to die. So she is carrying the Broken One inside her until he can be moved to a new stylus. If she dies, so does he."

"That is not good. We need his information." Paxton looked ready to panic. "I understood she was doing something to help him, but not what or how that help would be administered."

"Yeah, that's Storey all over. Now she's trying to fix the Louer and Toran problem."

Paxton looked at him sideways. "What problem?"

"She wants our people to share technology with the Louers. And she wants peace between the dimensions."

"They aren't my people." Paxton stared straight ahead. "I'm a Toran."

Eric sighed. "See that's the problem. There shouldn't be them and us. We were all the same at one time."

"But no longer."

"And that's wrong. We banished them and they suffered. Now they have a chance at a better life thanks to Storey and they need help to get started. They don't even have enough necessary food stores for the coming winter."

Paxton's lips thinned.

Eric grinned. "I'm warning you now, Storey won't let them suffer."

Paxton spun on his heels. "What does she expect us to do?"

"Help."

Paxton gasped. "They attacked us."

"Because they couldn't stay where they were any longer. When they found a way through…"

"That was Storey's fault. She opened a portal. If she hadn't done that…"

"You would never have found your brother, the Councilman would never have been put in a position to show his true colors and I'd have never met Storey." He smiled, a gentle twitch of his lips. "And that is something I wouldn't have wanted to miss."

"You can't keep her. You know that – right?" Paxton said slowly. "We have enough problems with just one dimension. There's no way we can handle dealing with multiple dimensions. That would be a political nightmare."

"I know that. But," he faced Paxton, "I have no intention of breaking off what's happening with her. I've spent all my life watching cold Toran relationships and wondering why none felt right for me. Now I've met Storey, I know. She's different. I saw her as a young girl when I first met her – only she wasn't. I was seeing what I expected to see. Not what she is – what she has become. She's a woman. She's become the star here. Not you or me or even the styluses. It's been her that has risen to the top of each challenge. I'm blessed to know her and I'll be incredibly lucky if she decides that I'm right for her – as I know she's right for me."

Paxton shook his head. "She can't keep going back and forth like this. It's going to cause problems."

"Maybe. But that door has been opened. We can't just ignore that." Eric shrugged. "I'm sure there's a way we can live in both dimensions. No one has to know. Just think of all I can learn. And Tammy is going to want to see Storey, too. And Storey will want to see her. Just think, the three of us can represent our worlds to each other."

Paxton's face puckered as he considered Eric's words. "Would Storey leave her world?"

Eric's eyebrows flew up. "She might. Particularly after her mother is gone. In the meantime, she'd certainly want to come back and forth. She's seen almost nothing of our world."

Just then, Storey's face filled the screen. "Eric? Paxton? Are you there?"

Paxton immediately tapped the keypad. "We are here."

As he tapped, the door opened and Toran council members and many others poured into his lab. Their voices raised in both outraged and terror.

"What has he done?"

"Are the Louers attacking?"

"What can we do?"

"Why has he been allowed to do this?"

Eric rounded on the last councilman who'd spoken, his temper flaring red once again. "He's done this because you people didn't believe Paxton and I. You let him loose. *You* gave him the means and methods to do this."

The group stopped and stared at each other. "We didn't think he'd do something so awful."

And Eric realized another truth. His people were as innocent as newborn babes. They'd handed over control, given complete power to his father and when he'd accepted it and made it his own, they were stunned. Now they felt betrayed. In truth, they should have seen it coming. He had. Storey certainly had.

"And...Paxton, is it true?" the elderly councilman

Marxel asked, his voice tremulous. "Are you really a Louer?"

Eric stepped in before his mentor could try and explain. "Paxton's family descended from the Louers." He smiled at them, his face grim, "As did we all. Remember that? Even the Councilman comes from Louers."

They all stared at each other, unsure of what to say. Who to listen to. Who to believe.

Then a woman stepped forward and brought the conversation around to the biggest issue.

"Is he still free?"

Eric didn't recognize the speaker, but the woman was tiny and wedged in-between several other women. He was happy to see them here. To see them sticking together and speaking up. He wouldn't be surprised if they'd been influenced by Storey's behavior to do so. Not that they'd had much of a chance to see her. But they'd have heard of her. And her exploits. These women could do so much more than they did. Storey would be good for them.

It was Storey that had opened his eyes.

"Is the human, Storey, coming back?" asked one of the woman.

"How can she?" said one grim faced male Eric didn't recognize. "The Councilman has ordered her death. Now he is trying to arrange an assassin to kill her."

"Are the Louers going to kill her? Paxton needs to help her."

The mass of questions and cries rose as each person set off another until Eric held up his hands. "Stop!"

Silence. Everyone looked at him, even Paxton, who said, "Eric, what do you suggest?"

"I suggest we take care of my father, and if that means sending him out to the fields as a laborer, then we do so."

"No." Paxton shook his head. "We can't trust him. Even out there he will find followers and rise up again."

Eric nodded, relieved that Paxton's words echoed his own thoughts.

"And he's sent many a prisoner to his death." Paxton added, "Or left them alone to exist in that horrible prison. He needs to experience the same isolation. Maybe after ten years, then he could work in the fields. Not now. He has to learn repentance."

Privately, Eric wasn't sure such a thing was possible. Maybe after a decade. He doubted it though. "And Storey?"

The cries were unanimous. "You have to go rescue her."

Eric waited to hear a dissent amongst them. Nothing. Neither did Paxton's vague origins appear to be more than a news item, quickly discarded as not important.

He smiled. "Good. But there is more to that." Just then Storey's face filled the monitor. Tammy was beside her. "Hi, Tammy," Eric said. He motioned the crowd to look at the monitor.

Several of them gasped and shrank back. Then Tammy smiled. A big toothy grin that made her more adorable than ever. "Everyone, this is Tammy. A Louer child that Storey saved from the old Louer dimension after my father banished Storey there secretly." Storey's face disappeared and then reappeared. This time she had Tammy in her arms.

Eric studied the group of Louer in the room standing behind Storey. He presumed they were looking at the motley group of Torans standing around him. His group showed mixed emotions at the sight of the Louer child in Storey's arms – or maybe it was the sight of all the Louers lined up behind her. Some showed shock, some understanding, some disgust, but there was a softening to their expressions.

Enough that he could see, with time, they'd come to understand the Louers were not so different.

Paxton tugged him back away from the crowd staring fascinated at the screen. He whispered beside him, "Do you see how they turn to you?"

He had, but figured it was just the situation.

"You have changed yourself, son. You've gone from a green ranger to a leader. Matured into a good man." He paused a moment, then said, "You should be proud of yourself."

Eric heard the quiet pride in Paxton's voice and smiled. "I guess I am at that."

He had changed. He might not be quite as far along the road as he might want, but he hadn't done anything that made him ashamed of his actions and that had to account for something. At least he knew value when he saw it. And Storey was valuable.

In a quiet voice, he said, "I still want Storey in my life."

"And we'll work on a way to make that happen."

Paxton's hand holding his stylus jerked. He raced over to his tablet where he'd left it on his desk. Immediately the stylus started writing. "They are ready to transfer the Broken One to a new stylus." Paxton read off. "Storey wants Eric there when it happens."

"Is it safe?"

"Yes. Especially now that your father is under guard." Paxton's head bobbed rapidly as he read the answer. He lifted his gaze to Eric. "Which stylus is the Broken One planning on being moved to?"

"To Storey's stylus." Eric smiled. "There really isn't much option at this point."

"Or we could move him to another stylus?" Paxton

frowned and raced to his box of styluses. He opened his box of styluses. "Which would be better?"

"I don't think we have a choice. It was done this way on purpose. Without Storey and her stylus, the process won't work. There's already a connection." Eric produced the broken stylus he'd removed from the box and had carried since, and replaced it into the box. "I guess it's a good thing I took that. I wonder if there are other styluses there that need help?"

Paxton's stylus jumped, sending him running back to his tablet. "Yes. They all need souls."

"And how do we do that?"

Paxton's hand once again twitched, the stylus apparently anxious to write the answer. "Once the Broken One is in his stylus he can coordinate the process. But souls are needed."

"Right." They were still at that balking point. They'd need some volunteers, and who would want that? He tabled the thought for the moment. There were other more immediate problems. "I need to go to the Louers' dimension."

"Good. You do that."

Just then the monitors on Paxton's workbench went crazy. Eric raced over and tapped the keypad, but nothing changed. Paxton nudged him gently aside. "Someone has initiated a cross-dimensional travel sequence on a codex." He studied the screen. "Using one of my spare codexes…"

"What? Who?"

Paxton's voice was grim. "I think it is your father. I'm checking the serial number." He clicked again. "It's one you brought back when you brought Tammy here. He must have grabbed it up before going to his chambers."

Unbelievable. Eric hadn't seen him touch anything, but

he'd been looking at the monitor, then wiping the screen clean at the time.

Paxton ran to the sideboard where his fingers tapped frantically on the keyboards. The monitor opened up on the Councilman's chambers. He turned back to stare at Eric. "He's knocked out his guards."

"But where can he go?" Eric strode to the monitor, staring at the forms of the two unconscious men. He'd thought he was past being surprised by anything his father did. Apparently not.

Paxton riffled through items on the top of his desk, then raced to his workbench. He turned back to Eric and the others, the color draining from his face. "He's got a pre-coded destination."

Eric stared at him, his mind racing through which of the codexes had been preset.

"Preset? To where?"

CHAPTER 26

STOREY LAY NERVOUSLY on a raised, flat surface. At least that's what she called it. She had no idea what *ipous* meant, but that's the word Tammy kept repeating as she tried to get Storey to lie down. Skorky's antics hadn't helped.

Potre sat on the side. And that made her feel a little more nervous than she could believe. Apparently the Broken One, Barrat, was a man of great importance to their people. He needed to survive. Hence the process she was about to undergo.

Still, she couldn't help but be a little nervous at the thought of what they might do to her afterwards. She wanted Eric. Someone needed to be on her side. To stand *for* her.

The process will not be difficult.

Broken One, are you sure you should be going into this stylus?

Yes.

My stylus? Are you sure you want Barrat in there with you?

We are honored.

Sure. Everyone was feeling honored…except her. In truth, she'd gotten accustomed to hearing and feeling the Broken One.

And for that we thank you. You have saved us, welcomed us, sheltered us. We are in your debt.

And now you need to move to the stylus. Fine. Let's get this done. She laid her head back down. Then lifted it again. *Are you sure you explained this to the Louers?*

Yes. They know what is going to happen.

Are they going to kill me once you have been saved?

No. They understand that you communicate with us. And with us, to them.

And that's okay? She hated to keep questioning every step, but the doubts kept her prodding. This was a little unnerving. *And they know about Eric coming?*

Eric has arrived.

Oh, thank God. Noises around her said that more people were arriving. In fact, the place had filled up to standing room only. Then she saw Eric. She smiled brightly. And her heart swelled with warmth. She loved that he'd hurried to be beside her.

"Storey." Eric rushed over to her side. "Are you okay?"

She laughed. "Definitely. And getting better now that you're here."

Just then he fell to his knees as Tammy jumped on him from behind. "Ris."

"Ooomph." But he was grinning. He grabbed the little girl, tugged her around to his chest and pulled her into his arms. He hugged her tight. Storey caught sight of Potre's face. The love in his gaze, the surprise and the acceptance. Eric closed his eyes and hugged Tammy tight.

Then she wiggled free and ran back to her father.

The stylus spoke. *It is time.*

Storey took a deep breath. *Then let's do it.*

She reached out, squeezed Eric's hand. And leaned back and closed her eyes.

Not so fast. Eric placed his hands on either side of her face, leaned down and kissed her. A tender, comforting, sample of so much more to come. Storey opened her eyes to see that wonderful gaze staring down at her. She wanted him. In her life, in her heart, in her soul. He was the other half of her. She'd traveled through dimensions to find him, and he'd traveled back the same way to help her.

They were meant to be together, and nothing, not even this, would stop that.

He smiled. "Now get this done so we can go have a cup of tea with your mother."

Storey brightened. "Thank you," she whispered. Then she leaned her head back. *Stylus, let's do this.*

Eric held her one hand and Tammy held her other. She smiled inside. *Thanks, Tammy.*

Torrey. Her name was said with such caring, tears came to Storey's eyes. Eric squeezed her hand – he'd seen her tears and worried. She whispered, "I'm fine."

"Good. Make sure you stay that way. I want lots of years with you."

"So do I."

The stylus spoke. *We need you to leave now.*

She started. *Leave and go where?*

Leave your body so that you aren't tugged into the stylus when we move the Broken One.

Crap that sounded so bad. But she'd forgotten how to do that. Her arm pulsed. Right, the honor marks.

Just think of them.

Ah, okay. In her mind's eye, she traced the marks. Instantly she was outside her body. She turned around to stare at the others. Everyone's eyes were glued to the transfer process in progress. There was an effervescent glow around her body. She didn't know if it was her own energy or that of the Broken One – or a product of the transfer process.

She turned around slowly, taking her time to study the room. Anything to take her mind off what was happening to her body.

The councilman flashed onto the screen, fine lines at the corner of his mouth, a sense of desperation in his eyes. Storey didn't recognize the room he was in. But he held a codex in his hands. As she watched, he clipped the unit on his wrist. She didn't know why he'd have one, but vaguely remembered seeing him snatch something off Paxton's desk. Then with one last hurried look around, he punched the large button. Immediately the black mist started at his feet.

He smiled, satisfaction oozing from his pores. Damn the man was smug. She didn't know if she dared say anything while the transfer was happening, but the stylus could multitask like no one else. She asked hesitantly, *Stylus?*

Yes.

She watched the smoke rise up the Councilman's face. It was too late to change anything now. *The Louers should be warned that they're about to have company.*

No. They aren't.

They aren't? I don't understand. The Councilman has a codex. He's travelling to one of the dimensions. He must be coming here.

Yes. He has taken one of Eric's codexes. Eric had spares when he came to rescue you In-between. Several were pre-coded to help him find you…just in case of trouble. On his return he gave them back to Paxton, putting them on the workbench. The Councilman slipped one into his pocket while he was looking at your message on the monitor.

She started. *I remember him seeing that message. Where are those preset coordinates going to take him?*

In-between.

She gasped in horror. Then in surprise. And finally at the justice of it all. *Oh my God. That is perfect.*

Dry humor lit the styluses' voice. *We thought so.*

She was still trying to grasp the truth of the Councilman's predicament when something shifted.

And then she was back in her body. She opened her eyes to see Eric's smiling face. She stretched up and kissed him.

Torrey! Tammy reached up and hugged her too.

Eric pulled back. "Are you okay?"

"Yes. I'm fine." And she was. In fact, she felt wonderful. "Stylus, how is the Broken One? Is he okay?"

When the answer didn't come immediately, she asked again. "Did he survive the transfer?" She frowned. Eric leaned closer. Tammy pulled back, her gaze flitting from Storey's face to Eric's. Then she tried to twist her features to match Eric's.

She had to laugh at their identical looks. Tammy was learning quickly.

"Is there still no answer?" Eric asked, his voice tense.

They waited in silence for several long minutes.

We are here.

"Yes." Storey gave a fist bump in the air. Just to confirm, she had to ask, "So the Broken One is fine now?"

He is. Now we are fine.

Perfect.

And it was.

ERIC WATCHED STOREY'S approach to her house. They'd left immediately after the transfer, the Louers giving her a rousing send off. Efforts to create a workable truce between Paxton and Tammy's father were in progress. The Louers were ecstatic that Storey had saved the Broken One. Apparently that, more than any promises made, had convinced them of her sincerity.

That and her new honor marks.

Eric knew they were for saving the stylus, who needed souls, and for saving Barrat, who needed a stylus. There might even be a few extra curls in there for having made peace with the Louers. He didn't know. Tammy had seen them. The other Louers had definitely seen them. They'd spoken amongst each other and pointed at her the whole time. Typical Storey, she'd been oblivious.

Now he wondered how long it would take her to realize the marks traveled up her neck and down her back. If she kept this up, she'd be covered from head to toe.

Considering she wore them so well, he wouldn't mind in the least.

She was such an honorable person. So not like his father. That his father had done himself in was something he couldn't quite get out of his mind.

It was fitting.

Eric didn't know if there was anything they could do to help him. At least at this point. Not that anyone seemed to care. He knew he didn't dare go back In-between to save him.

Storey turned back and motioned at him. "Aren't you coming?"

"I just thought you'd like to see for yourself, first." He smiled down at her.

She turned to stare at her house. "I do. But I'd like you there with me."

Nice. He'd helped her put on a sweater earlier, not wanting the honor marks to show – at least initially. She had enough to deal with without trying to explain the unexplainable right away.

He knew she'd do fine regardless of what they found in her dimension, but he hoped for her sake, her world was back the way it should be.

He held out his hand and together they approached the house they'd raided endless times. "It looks the same."

"Yes," she said, "It does. And that worries me."

"Front door or back?"

"Kitchen door."

They walked around to the back and stepped onto the porch. "I'm so glad to be back."

The door opened in front of them. Storey's mother smiled and opened her arms.

Storey ran into her mother's embrace.

At this point, Eric didn't think she cared which mother it was.

CHAPTER 27

"I WAS SO afraid you'd not have gotten my message." Her mother kissed Storey's cheek. "It was all so crazy with the festivities, the people I met – one in particular – and the wild weather. It seems like every time I managed to call home, you were out." Her mother shook her head and tugged Storey inside. "I'm so glad that's all over and we're back together again." Her mother glanced over at Eric. "How nice to see you again too, Eric." She motioned to the table. "Come. Sit down."

Storey cast a questioning look back at Eric. He shrugged. Storey sat down at the kitchen table. She glanced around. It looked wonderful. It looked like home.

"I'm so sorry. I wasn't supposed to be gone so long. The ceremony lasted all weekend, and…" she blushed, "I met someone there. And given who it was, I needed to stay and work through a few things. And of course with all that weird weather, and highways being closed, well… I stayed. Still, I hadn't expected to be gone so long." She leaned forward earnestly. "I did try to call several times, but the crazy weather had service out all around the country.

Weird weather? Closed highways? No phone service? Storey exchanged a long look with Eric, knowing it was most likely the time twists and portal tears that had caused all the damage. And then she remembered the festival. There'd been special festivities planned that weekend. She was stunned. Everything that had happened to her had taken only a couple of days, even though it seems like weeks or months. If she'd been here, she would hardly have seen her mother anyway.

"And who did you meet at the ceremonies?" Storey asked cautiously, still trying to figure out if her mother had been aware at all of her absence.

Her mother smiled, a little lopsided, a little insecure, but sweet. She glanced between Storey and Eric then back to Storey. She took a deep breath. "I didn't expect this. I'd never imagined…after all this time." She reached out and grabbed Storey's hand and sat down beside her. "I don't know how to tell you this, and with Eric here…but…well…I have to tell you." The words burst out in an excited, girlish torrent. "I met your father."

Storey jerked. Her gaze met Eric's. *Her father?* Her thoughts spun on the possibilities. Time twisting. Dimensions trying to reestablish balance…was this real…?

Her stylus spoke quietly in the back of her mind.

This is real. Balance returning for all.

"And…" she asked cautiously, shocked and yet, intrigued.

Her mother's excited voice bubbled over. "I know this is sudden. Maybe it's good that Eric is here. You can talk with him." She took a deep breath and barreled forward. "He would like to get to know you," her face pleaded for acceptance, "if you're open to the idea. We talked. About our past. The mess we'd made of our lives since. Our relationship. Like really talked. And…" she took another deep breath, as if not believing this herself, "We've started…well, you know…seeing each other."

r mother sat back, a worried look on her face. "But he's

concerned about how you'll feel."

STOREY SHUT DOWN for a moment. Shock was too mild a word to describe what she was feeling. Stupefied might be better. If that was a word. Yet, inside, with all that had happened, she had to wonder. She's been so torn over her father's presence in the other dimension, so confused over her own emotions, this just seemed too bizarre.

Maybe her parents were being offered a second chance.

That, she hadn't expected. When the dimensions shifted, she'd had a pang of regret for what could never be with her father. And now here was the opportunity again.

And this time, her father wanted back in *her* life?

Had she created this? And did it matter?

No and no.

She smiled at her stylus's answer. Eric's silent support made her want to laugh and cry at the same time. She wanted to rage at him and hug him. To laugh and scream a million questions. Yet none would form in her head.

"I don't know what to say." She tried to speak her words carefully, not wanting to upset her mother, but not knowing how she felt herself. She had to find a way forward. Somehow.

"Then don't say anything. We're going to take it slow," her mother promised. "This isn't about him or me. This is about us."

She smiled. "Now, how about a cup of tea."

Tea. Her mother's answer to everything. She watched her mother bustle about the kitchen, putting on the kettle. Probably to give Storey some time to process the huge bombshell she'd just dumped on her.

Eric took the chair her mother had been sitting in. She leaned closer and whispered, "I can't help but think this happened because of us."

"Or maybe we just made it happen faster." He tilted his head to look at her closer. "Is it so bad?"

She frowned, considering it. Then shrugged. "I don't know."

He turned slightly to look at her mother, then glanced back at Storey. "Your mother appears happy. Young almost."

That was true, and after all she'd been through, Storey knew how important happiness was. She studied the dreamy look in her mother's face and smiled.

Storey had found someone, so why shouldn't her mother find someone? And if that someone ended up being her father…maybe that *was* a good thing – for everyone.

It would certainly change things. But then, as she'd found, change could be good – very good.

Just then her mother, from deep inside the fridge, popped her head out and asked, "Storey, do you know what happened to the cheese?"

Storey gasped, looked over at Eric wide eyed and the two broke out laughing.

In fact, the world looked damn bright all over.

Author's Note

Thank you for reading Darkest Designs! If you enjoyed my book, I'd appreciate it if you'd leave a review.

Dear reader,

I love to hear from readers, and you can contact me at my website: www.dalemayer.com or at my Facebook author page. To be informed of new releases and special offers, sign up for my newsletter or follow me on BookBub. And if you are interested in joining Dale Mayer's Reader Group, here is the Facebook sign up page.
http://geni.us/DaleMayerFBGroup

Cheers,
Dale Mayer

Gem Stone (A Gemma Stone Mystery)

A juvie kid trying to stay on the right path stumbles into trouble...

Gemma takes her camera everywhere. From juvie hall to a halfway home, the new hobby gives her a focus she'd never had before and... hope in a future. Until she takes pictures of something that could get her killed.

And not just her...after she and another juvie girl are chased by a stranger to the halfway home that same night, the other girl goes missing and Gemma knows she needs help. But who can she trust?

Not the authorities that's for sure. Trusting them is impossible for a girl with her damaged history, and besides, who cares about a troubled kid...especially when trouble just naturally seems to find her.

In Cassie's Corner

Faith and loyalty are tested as a young girl learns what it is to believe – in herself, in her friends, and in life after death.

Cassie's best friend, bad boy Todd, is gone. Gone as in dead. Gone as in he's now a ghost.

But she doesn't realize that when he wakes her in her bedroom and begs her not to believe what they say about him. It's not until the next day when her parents tell her about the accident that she learns the truth…

The police believe Todd was living up to the family name, drinking and driving and coming to a predictable end. It's up to her to find out the truth and clear his name.

Todd is shocked at his sudden change in circumstances…and angry. He struggles with his new ghostly reality, realizing all he's lost as he watches his brother build a relationship with Cassie as the two pair up to find out what really happened to him.

The truth isn't always pretty, and Cassie has to be stronger than ever before. Especially when the whole world seems to be against her.

About the Author

Dale Mayer is a *USA Today* best-selling author, best known for her SEALs military romances, her Psychic Visions series, and her Lovely Lethal Garden cozy series. Her contemporary romances are raw and full of passion and emotion (Broken But … Mending, Hathaway House series). Her thrillers will keep you guessing (Kate Morgan, By Death series), and her romantic comedies will keep you giggling (*It's a Dog's Life*, a stand-alone novella; and the Broken Protocols series, starring Charming Marvin, the cat).

Dale honors the stories that come to her—and some of them are crazy, break all the rules and cross multiple genres!

To go with her fiction, she also writes nonfiction in many different fields, with books available on résumé writing, companion gardening, and the US mortgage system. All her books are available in print and ebook format.

Connect with Dale Mayer Online

Dale's Website – www.dalemayer.com
Twitter – @DaleMayer
Facebook Page – geni.us/DaleMayerFBFanPage
Facebook Group – geni.us/DaleMayerFBGroup
BookBub – geni.us/DaleMayerBookbub
Instagram – geni.us/DaleMayerInstagram
Goodreads – geni.us/DaleMayerGoodreads
Newsletter – geni.us/DaleNews

Also by Dale Mayer

Published Adult Books:

Psychic Vision Series

Tuesday's Child

Hide'n Go Seek

Maddy's Floor

Garden of Sorrow

Knock, Knock…

Rare Find

Eyes to the Soul

Now You See Her

Shattered

Into the Abyss

Psychic Visions Books 1–3

Psychic Visions Books 4–6

Psychic Visions Books 7–9

By Death Series

Touched by Death – Part 1

Touched by Death – Part 2

Touched by Death – Parts 1&2

Haunted by Death

Chilled by Death

By Death Books 1–3

Second Chances...at Love Series

Second Chances – Part 1

Second Chances – Part 2

Second Chances – complete book (Parts 1 & 2)

Charmin Marvin Romantic Comedy Series

Broken Protocols

Broken Protocols 2

Broken Protocols 3

Broken Protocols 3.5

Broken Protocols 1-3

Broken and... Mending

Skin

Scars

Scales (of Justice)

Broken but... Mending 1-3

Glory

Genesis

Tori

Celeste

Glory Trilogy

Biker Blues

Biker Blues: Morgan, Part 1

Biker Blues: Morgan, Part 2

Biker Blues: Morgan, Part 3

Biker Baby Blues: Morgan, Part 4

Biker Blues: Morgan, Full Set

Biker Blues: Salvation, Part 1

Biker Blues: Salvation, Part 2

Biker Blues: Salvation, Part 3

Biker Blues: Salvation, Full Set

SEALs of Honor

Mason: SEALs of Honor, Book 1

Hawk: SEALs of Honor, Book 2

Dane: SEALs of Honor, Book 3

Swede: SEALs of Honor, Book 4

Shadow: SEALs of Honor, Book 5

Cooper: SEALs of Honor, Book 6

Markus: SEALs of Honor, Book 7

Evan: SEALs of Honor, Book 8

Mason's Wish: SEALs of Honor, Book 9

SEALs of Honor, Books 1–3

SEALs of Honor, Books 4–6

Collections

Dare to Be You…

Dare to Love…

Dare to be Strong…

RomanceX3

Standalone Novellas

It's a Dog's Life

Riana's Revenge

Published Young Adult Books:

Family Blood Ties Series

Vampire in Denial

Vampire in Distress

Vampire in Design

Vampire in Deceit

Vampire in Defiance

Vampire in Conflict

Vampire in Chaos

Vampire in Crisis

Vampire in Control

Vampire in Charge

Family Blood Ties Set 1–3

Family Blood Ties Set 1–5

Family Blood Ties Set 4–6

Family Blood Ties Set 7–9

Sian's Solution – A Family Blood Ties Short Story

Design series

Dangerous Designs

Deadly Designs

Darkest Designs

Design Series Trilogy

Standalone

In Cassie's Corner

Gem Stone (a Gemma Stone Mystery)

Time Thieves

Published Non-Fiction Books:

Career Essentials

Career Essentials: The Résumé

Career Essentials: The Cover Letter

Career Essentials: The Interview

Career Essentials: 3 in 1